STANDING
AT THE
CROSSROADS

CHARLES DAVIS

STANDING AT THE CROSSROADS

The Permanent Press
Sag Harbor, NY 11963

For information, address:
  The Permanent Press
  4170 Noyac Road
  Sag Harbor, NY 11963
  www.thepermanentpress.com

Library of Congress Cataloging-in-Publication Data

  Davis, Charles–
    Standing at the crossroads / Charles Davis.
       p. cm.
    ISBN 978-1-57962-213-8 (alk. paper)
       1. Self-actualization—Fiction. 2. Regression (Civilization)—
    Fiction. 3. Walking—Fiction. 4. Storytelling—Fiction. 5. Books
    and reading—Fiction. I. Title.

  PR6104.A88S73 2011
  823'.92—dc22   2010044082

Printed in the United States of America.

For Jeannette and all that equatorial jazz

ACKNOWLEDGEMENTS

Several images in this novel were inspired by Alberto Manguel's magnificent *A History of Reading* (Flamingo, 1997), a work that stimulated many more fancies eventually discarded in the interests of balance. It is a book that every reader should have on their shelves.

My thanks to Phil, who delighted me by recognizing paradise, Laura for faith when faith was failing, Marty for treating commercial sense with a fine disdain, and Judith for changing her mind.

OK, let's go, please.

Call me Ishmael. That's not my name, but you can call me that. I am a type of Ishmael. I do not mean an outsider. Africans are defined by belonging, not isolation. But I am a witness, taking with words what would not be taken by other means.

Picture this. There is a man standing at a crossroads. Beside him, a woman. Behind them, a child. They are surrounded by men on horses. The men have guns in their hands and God in their hearts. They are the Warriors of God and they believe in perfection. Man, woman, and child have no weapons, no faith, only a story.

OK, let's go, please.

❋ ❋ ❋

I first see Kate at the souk. She is sitting on a bench in front of the *chai* shop. The Warriors of God are in front of the government rest house with their horses and the Landcruiser. We have many men with guns and horses, more since the drill was blown up. The Warriors of God are drinking cold things. Kate is peering at her cell phone, so absorbed that it would seem she has lost something inside it. I should leave. Jemal's men are no friends of mine. But I need new books and the foreigners have always given books for my library. They like to picture their novels crossing the desert on my back. So I walk toward the white woman.

Souk is the word we use, but it is not the sort of souk featured in tomes of travelers' tales full of color, bustle, copper kettles, spices, and bolts of bright cloth. Our souk is not like that. It is a thing of dust and dry beans and sacks of sorghum and powdered milk, 'A gift from the EC,' sold by Idris the Madman, who dreams of islands. Sometimes we can buy tomatoes, sometimes only bread, sometimes not even that. There is *chai* and Coca-Cola, occasionally cold things, always people. With the camps full, the souk is a place of meeting, refuge and flight, but no commerce is done, or not the commerce of small moneys. There may be talk of mining, of minerals and oil, of guns and gold, but the business is the business of Business, not people.

"Excuse me, madam. May I be permitted to speak with you for one moment, please?"

Kate looks up, a little startled. It is sometimes this way. I have been told by other white people that I speak too formally, my language dated like the writers on whom it has been modeled. I have, at least, learned not to ask to have intercourse with them. That does not work at all. It would seem that that which was once communication has dwindled to mere coition in the modern world.

She does not reply, yet watches me in a manner that suggests assent. She is a short woman, with a strong face and steady eyes that do no dance of etiquette, but hold your gaze, as if candor is respect. Her time in my country cannot have been easy. Propriety is important here and deference is valued more than honesty.

I explain my purpose, ask her for old paperbacks, careful to display the forms of courtesy that I have learned from the novels of Mr. Trollope and Mr. Galsworthy. When my speech is finished, she says she has heard of me, The Barefoot Librarian. The way she says it, the words sound like the title of a book, one she would perhaps like to read or that has been recommended by a fellow reader, but she does not elaborate.

I wait, not wishing to seem importunate.

She waits, too, watching me with a cool, distant curiosity, the degree of which I cannot yet determine. It is always a delicate moment, the period between request and bequest, for it is then that potential donors decide whether to fob me off with a token contribution or really try to help.

Still she does not speak.

Africans are good at waiting, but this silence is not normal for white people. White people do not like silence. In their books, they call it pregnant. They fear silence is the prologue to something that will grow beyond regulation.

Yet Kate says nothing.

Simply waits and watches, her figure partially obscured by my shadow, a slender ghost that slouches over her knees and folds itself across the far corner of the bench. Her own shadow is distorted by the wall of the *chai* shop, twisted awkwardly, an unfamiliar creature trying to fit itself into an incommodious space not fashioned for it by nature.

I explain again what I need and why.

Abruptly, she loses interest or patience, I do not know which, or appears to, at least, says quietly but firmly: "I don't read novels. I only have time for what is true."

White people do not normally shock me. I have read their books and told their stories very many times. I understand them, have seen the places that made them, seen the lives they want to live, all in the reading and rereading and retelling. Sometimes my people call me 'doctor,' for though my skin is dark, my mind is pale. But when Kate suggests fiction is not true she shocks me very much. Stories get nearer to the truth than facts.

"I'm sorry," says Kate, mistaking my dismay for the discomfort her directness must often cause my compatriots. "I'm busy. I must make a call. But there's no coverage at the moment."

She inspects her cell phone again, dismissing me by taking refuge in technology. I later learn that she has collected many facts about my country—dates, names, numbers, places—but she does not read them right. Otherwise, she would know that when the cell phones stop working, it means someone, somewhere is about to die, and the killers do not want word to spread. Words, even simple words of warning, are powerful. That is one reason why the men with guns and horses hate me, for words tied into stories are words they cannot curb by shutting down a satellite.

Jemal appears behind his men, stepping carefully across the broken boards of the rest house verandah. He looks at me. We were together in the orphanage, but there is no kindness between us now. He will kill me one day. He has told me this. But it will not be today, I think. He turns aside, speaks brief words in the language of the north, and the Warriors of God get ready to ride into the desert.

※   ※   ※

The books I carried on my back have rubbed into my flesh and bones. Sometimes they leak out again. At night, falling asleep, I often dream I am reading. The book is in my hand, a known book by a known writer, I can feel its weight, I can see the words, and I am reading, and the way the words fit together matches the way the writer fits words together. Then I turn the page and the words make no sense or the page repeats itself, so I go back to the beginning and start again. But when I turn the page once more, the same thing happens, over and over again, until I wake and realize that there is no book in my hand, and my reading is nothing but a dream.

I dream books in the waking world, too, willing them into being as I walk between villages, so that I am in sort walking with the characters from my books, picturing them at my side. Sometimes their presence is so strong that it even inflects the rhythm of my own walking. With Captain Ahab, for instance, I do not walk quickly, but I keep going for a very long time and rarely rest. His progress is hampered by his ivory leg sinking into the soft sand, but he ploughs on regardless, because he cannot relax and fears that, once stopped, he will never start again. Miss Havisham is slower than a government paycheck. Her dress is not suited to the *qoz* and she is a very old lady. She protests most bitterly, until I become peevish like her, and end up bickering with myself about which path to take. By contrast, Lizzie Bennet does not complain about the heat and dust, but walks steadily, holding her skirts clear of her ankles when crossing thickets of thorny grass, so that we proceed smoothly in a most pleasant concord of mutual sympathy. Huckleberry Finn is a cheerfully unruly companion, darting back and forth, talking all the time, trying to spend his inexhaustible energy. His is a nervous search for a world in which he will be free and safe, as if the two can be found together. Don Quijote is congenial, but erratic. He is always seeking enemies to challenge— like Kate, as I will discover shortly. Steerforth is a bit wet. Barkis is willing.

Perhaps my choice of reading seems outlandish for this hot, landlocked place? But like all good things, my library was made by chance not choice, compiled through the impulsive generosity of strangers: consular officials, NGO field workers, foreign teachers and contract personnel, these have been my stockpilers, supplying the raw material of the road on which I walk. Thus I tell tales of oceans my listeners have never seen, of strange countries and alien rituals they will never know, and conflicts that must be retailored to match the fabric of their experience. But it is right that I bring them a world they do not know. Books should be written and read out of context. Only then do they properly engage the imagination. Mr. Melville wrote a story about a whale, but it was a book about the whole world, and he wrote it in front of a window in front of a mountain in the middle of Maine.

My own book must be a love story, a poem to people, and a celebration of the power of words.

Yet I am telling a story of war, flight and murder.

❊   ❊   ❊

Two days pass. I find no new books. I must take a place on the truck that is due to leave for Al Asher. It is too dangerous to walk now. It is dangerous to travel at all, but if you take the risk, it is best done in company. This is Africa: life is community and where there is no community there is no life; that is why they destroy the villages.

I will get off the truck at the crossroads and go to the well of books. Al Asher is safe, but it is not good for books anymore because very many consulates have closed and those that remain are bureaus of business rather than culture. I might be given the odd dog-eared spy novel or a spine-cracked Penguin classic, but not enough to remake a library, even a portable one. This will be my third trip to the well of books.

I stocked the well when the war got big again and the commercial agents withdrew and the consular libraries closed, abandoning all disposable printed matter. All disposable printed matter meant everything that did not contain a commercial or diplomatic secret, which is to say everything that might be interesting to a man like me. While other people fought over office furnishings and copper pipes, I foraged for books. I found very many volumes, so many that I could not store them all in Anahud. Instead, I took them to the crossroads.

The older paperbacks were falling apart, but I wrapped the newer books in plastic and stacked them in the wide mouth of the shallow well. The well is dry and nobody goes there for water now. Few even notice the low rim of sun-baked bricks. I left the broken paperbacks in the camps, distributing blocks of pages at random. They are good firelighters, but I like to imagine someone making a new story from the fragments they find. That is the way of reading: reading people, places, books, we are always piecing together patchy information and trying to make a pattern from it. That was what Kate was doing, taking snapshots of my country and trying to make a pattern. Sometimes the patterns we make are better than the pattern the author intended. Sometimes they are simply wrong.

I see her for the second time on my way to the truck park. She is in an alley off the main street. I say 'alley' and 'street,' but there are no alleys or streets here, only ways stabilized by use, and even they may disappear if somebody builds a house in the gap. But these spaces serve a similar purpose to the passages that other people in other places call alleys and streets. My country is not well made for conventional representation. I am thinking of the European maps that purport to show the infrastructure of this place. They are works of marvelous fantasy, locating straight roads where ways a mile wide meander across the *qoz* and 'restaurants' where a *chai* shack sometimes serves brown beans with roundels of flat grey bread. Like the mapmakers, I am telling a story using signs that can only approximate what I am describing. Forgive me. I am pedantic. But these days, words are my only resource—words and you.

Kate is in a narrow alley off the main street. There are no doorways, only two long mud walls, no exits save at either end of the alley. At its further end, there is a man, and between Kate and myself, two more. They are walking at her, talking angry words, saying insults she cannot understand. They are Warriors of God, nomads who have always raided villages in search of cattle, and who now raid in search of money and God. Like everyone else, they are trying to survive in a world that has changed, adapting what they know to the new world.

Kate is standing still in the middle of the alley. She is in trouble. She is scared. But she hides it well. And she is beautiful. Her features are regular, unnaturally symmetrical. She has a broad brow and large eyes, wide and widely spaced, and dark hair that defines her face with sharp lines. But most beautiful is the way she stands, the way she looks—stubborn, watching the men defiantly. She is vulnerable yet independent, even at the cost of safety. Beauty may be found in the happenstance of flesh and bone, but it must be quickened by more than blood if it is to move us.

Kate's courage moves me.

It moves me into the alley.

I know what these men want. They want to punish her for the unspoken crime of being a woman. It is the easiest way they can find to fight their own fears. Kate knows enough to wear a loose dress with long sleeves and skirts that reach below her knees, but her hair is showing. Time before, this was allowed in a white woman, but not now. Too much has changed, the world become too fragile, to permit exceptions. They will probably not hurt her badly. Not a foreigner, not here in the town. But you never know with men who are practiced in the incisive art of unwomaning a woman's body.

I should walk on, but I do not because I know that time to come these men will kill me like they have killed so many others before, and it pleases me to upset them while I live. They are walking at Kate, talking angry words, when the man at the far end of the alley sees me, and warns his companions, who turn to face this new threat. They do not have their guns, but they will have knives strapped to their upper arms, knives with a ridge along the flat of the blade so that the wound will not heal cleanly. I have big shoulders and strong arms, the muscles made abnormally large by the many years of carrying books, and I learned how to fight well enough in the orphanage. I could beat them, I believe, even three of them. But if beating is necessary, it is better to beat a man's spirit than his body. Bodies heal quicker than the spirit. Besides, when the world is nonsensical, nonsense is one of the few defenses left to a poor man. Nonsense, walking, reading, and, in the end, when nothing else is left, writing.

I take out the book, open it at the page that pleases so many children and those adults who have kept the better part of childishness in their hearts. Everyone has childishness inside them, childishness often made ugly by age, but the love of nonsense is a beautiful thing. I raise the book and the Warriors of God look troubled for they do not like books being raised against them. Warriors of God do not like people reading. It is a power they cannot control. That is why they want me dead. It is the reason they persecute women, too. They fear women. Women and books are stronger than them. Women and books possess secret, private places in which they worry some occult and unfathomable mischief is being done. Happily, they are right.

I begin to read aloud, reciting really. I know these words well, but the book is a weapon of sorts in itself.

> 'Twas brillig, and the slithy toves
>   Did gyre and gimble in the wabe:
> All mimsy were the borogoves,
>   And the mome raths outgrabe.
>
> "Beware the Jabberwock, my son!
>   The jaws that bite, the claws that catch!
> Beware the Jujub bird, and shun
>   The frumious Bandersnatch!"

He took his vorpal sword in hand:
    Long time the manxome foe he sought—
So rested he by the Tumtum tree,
    And stood awhile in thought.

And, as in uffish thought he stood,
    The Jabberwock, with eyes of flame,
Came whiffling through the tulgey wood,
    And burbled as it came!

One two! One two! And through and through
    The vorpal blade went snicker-snack!
He left it dead, and with its head
    He went galumphing back.

"And hast thou slain the Jabberwock?
    Come to my arms, my beamish boy!
O frabjous day! Callooh! Callay!"
    He chortled in his joy.

'Twas brillig, and the slithy toves
    Did gyre and gimble in the wabe:
All mimsy were the borogoves,
    And the mome raths outgrabe.

I have seen the magic these words make on children
and reason that children's magic will not go well with these
men, for the child in them is the child of fear, not the child
of nonsense. At first, the Warriors of God step forward to
fight me, but they falter when they hear the Jubjub bird
and Bandersnatch, and by the time the Jabberwock comes
whiffling through the tulgey wood, the two men in front are
glancing uncertainly at one another. The vorpal blade goes
snicker-snack and they back off, so that Kate is between
them and the beamish boy. It is the Callooh! Callay! that
finishes them. They flee, terrified that some triumphant

and terrible spell is being cast. 'Twas brillig, and the slithy toves did gyre and gimble in the wabe: all mimsy were the borogoves, and the mome raths outgrabe. Perhaps they are right.

At first, Kate is incredulous, which is as it should be with nonsense, but then she starts to laugh and it is the most frabjous sound I have heard since I was in the camps. You would be surprised how often people laugh in the camps. Displaced, dispossessed, hungry, risking rape or castration when they venture beyond the perimeter, yet still they laugh. Laughter and tears ghost one another. Laughter can make tears of joy and tears of pain can make a face like laughter. Either way, life is made more bearable, and we find the strength to carry on. Kate's laughter is the laughter of one who wants to live long and well. She even snorts, her glee so immoderate that it must have a second outlet.

I warm to this strange woman. I have loved a good number of women, loved them well, I hope, for they deserved it, and in doing so I have committed another misdeed in the eyes of the Warriors of God, since the love and loving of women is not admissible in their wing-clipped version of the world. But despite the many wives I had in the days when I walked from village to village, the immediacy and artlessness of the feeling I have for this laughing, snorting woman is as alien as the place she comes from—or would be were it not for the books that have made her place familiar to me and made old companions of many strange sensations. Full of reading, I am on friendly terms with both that which is foreign to my experience and that which is foreign to my nature. Like all lovers of books, I have become a kind of library myself, and need only consult the various volumes lodged inside me to make, at the very least, some small sense of what would otherwise seem unknowable.

"You still want books?" she says when, at length, she has mastered her laughter.

"I still want books, madam. But this was not done for books."

"Please, do not call me madam. My name is Kate."

"Yes, Miss Kate." A brief expression of distaste crosses her face, I do not know why. "Miss Kate, we should not linger here. It is dangerous. Please to follow me."

The Battle of Jabberwocky, as Kate later calls it, is an easy victory given what happens afterwards, but I know my enemies. The Warriors of God are simple men, but they understand the power of words. They believe that words in an amulet will guard against the evil eye, that learning their book by heart will guarantee them a place in paradise, even that declaiming the beautiful names of God can protect them from the weapons of other men. But words can harm them, too. The men in the alley understand enough to know that Jabberwocky is made of words they cannot control because they are words without meaning. They are frightened by what they cannot control. That is why they kill.

For my part, I have long lived in words, perhaps too long, and know all too well their uses and abuses. Words connect, but they can also keep people out. Some books do not tell a story, but build a wall of words shielding the reader from the world, imprisoning as they protect. Sometimes though, words are a necessary defense. They are a poor weapon, a hit and miss magic, and in this place you only have to miss once and you are dead, or as good as, but they are the only weapon most of us have.

The slithy toves did gyre and gimble in the wabe.

❖ ❖ ❖

We are sitting on a truck at the edge of the souk. Kate, myself and a score of other hopeful travelers. I told her she should leave Anahud and she said she was leaving anyway, had been going to fetch her bag. I did not expect her to take the truck, but she has no automobile of her own and travels like one of us: on foot, on donkeys, on top of a merchant's wares. This is a good truck, loaded with sacks of *dura*, so we will sleep well tonight, and tomorrow if the way is slow. It will be crowded, though. Transport is scarce and there are many who wish to escape the conflict. More people are arriving all the time.

A Landcruiser crosses the square and stops behind our vehicle. The crowd continues scrambling up the slatted sides of the truck, thrusting bags into the hands of waiting relatives. They are so eager to get away that they do not notice Jemal emerging from the Landcruiser. No curtain of stillness falls, there is no show of meekness, just the pushy agitation of people desperate to escape. He ignores them and walks around to where Kate and I are sitting. She has covered her hair with a long scarf that she can also pull across her mouth, not for modesty, but against the dust.

He looks up at us, then says: "This is your woman?"

Kate regards him with scorn, but he will not look at her directly, will not sully himself in this way. He merely repeats his question. It is a habit he has had since childhood, repeating himself as if language is ritual, a formal procedure that does not so much describe the world as codify it, making it fit a pattern acceptable to his expectations. It is a foolish habit and this is a foolish question. He knows Kate cannot be my woman and I cannot claim to be an approved guardian protecting my charge. Even if she was a woman who could be possessed and was possessed by me, I could not say it. Not now, not here. A black man with a white woman would not be permitted. Race is patrilineal, which is why the Warriors of God rape the women when they destroy the villages, to destroy the race, too. Any child will be Semitic, not Hamitic. It is a nonsense, of course, not the playful nonsense of Mr. Carroll, but a nonsense of feeling rather than meaning. Even Jemal with his milk-coffee complexion has African blood running in his veins. I know where he comes from. But it is a nonsense I cannot fight except perhaps in words and stories.

"She is not my woman."

Jemal watches me, his eyes darting across my face as if searching for some familiar feature that has gone missing. For one misguided, hopeful moment, I wonder whether he has not been touched by some memory of the past, and is consequently endeavoring to give me an excuse for defying his men, pretending I really am her *muharram*. As it is, merely being with her is risky. We are clearly not related and the morality laws can be read in any manner that pleases the men in power, which is to say the men with guns and horses. Whatever the text, be it a book, a body, or a landscape, how it is read can change everything.

"You scared my men with your magic," he says. It is an accusation, not a statement of fact. Though the recollection of his accomplices' panic pleases me, I do not smile. Smiling is not wise with Jemal. But a snort escapes Kate. He glances at her sharply, stung by her derision, then turns away from her with equal haste, as if the sight of her face is more hurtful than the sound of her ridicule. Maybe it is for him. He never did get a grip on womankind, a failure on his part that is hard to forgive. Had he got a grip on womankind, he might not have clung onto God so closely.

"Your men were trying to scare me," says Kate.

Jemal ignores her, repeats his accusation.

"It was a poem," I say, "a simple poem," though there is no such thing as a 'simple' poem. Even a bad poem, and Jabberwocky is not a bad poem, can say many complex things if it is read correctly, for there is as much poetry in the reading as in the writing. Jemal is right to call it magic.

He says nothing, only stares at me, and I can feel all the love we had for one another turned to hate. But even if he did not hate me, for fear of words, he and his men would want to kill me. And they are right to want to kill me. If I was them, I would want to kill me, too. But as they say in England (I have read this expression and I like it very much), *mustn't grumble*. The Warriors of God want to kill everyone, after all, everyone who does not, by virtue of skin, sex and faith, fit the perfection they seek. They are very killing people.

❂ ❂ ❂

Everybody scratches their bottom from time to time, but some people feel compelled to sniff their finger afterwards. Fr. Gianni was a sniffer, always scratching under his skirts then inhaling the holy aroma of piety. It was not so much his self he smelled as the sweet scent of sanctity emanating from a life sacrificed to a mission in the middle of nowhere. At the time, I did not understand this. And he did not understand me. We hated each other.

When my father was killed, a woman called Jenny came to see us. She gave my mother flour, rice and beans. She gave me a book called *Tricycle Tim*. It was about a boy with a tricycle who was looking for a man called Mr. Nobody who lived Nowhere. Except for the hand-pedaled carts of the legless men, I had never seen a tricycle, nor a house like Mr. Nobody's house with very many levels and very big windows. But that did not matter, because I believed in this Nowhere place, where Mr. Nobody had boarded over the stairs, turning his house into a playground for children with tricycles. Reading the story of how Tricycle Tim tracked down Mr. Nobody and the heady account of his first wild ride from the top of the house to the bottom, I forgot all about my own problems and lost myself in the boy's carefree joy. I had discovered the magic of books, that they can turn Nowhere into Somewhere and make Nobody Somebody and show that Everybody is Somebody. I still liked the tales told by the elders, but this book story was special because it was private and did not happen unless I made it happen. I read *Tricycle Tim* so often that I could recite it whole or continue the story from any given sentence. I still can.

Jenny kept giving me books, some written for children, others abridged for adult learners, until I was living more on books than on USAID rice and Canada Aid Soy Milk. *Moby Dick*, *A High Wind in Jamaica*, *Jane Eyre*, *Great Expectations* . . . I was born beside an African swamp, but I lived on the oceans and in the English countryside because I was happier inside a Simplified Reader than out. Then the war came back, bringing hunger and disease. The white people left, my mother died, and I began to walk, walking north because that was where the books came from, walking north looking for Nowhere.

I met Jemal in the grasslands beyond the swamp. Nearly every living thing had been eaten, but one day I chanced upon a sickly looking chicken sheltering in the shade of a burned hut. As I was stalking the bird, I spotted another boy stealthily approaching from the other side of the hut. He saw me and the bird saw us and we rushed at the bird and threw ourselves at it and each caught a leg. We lay there, face to face, the bird between us, holding our respective legs, watching each other watching the bird watching us. Nothing was said, but we knew the energy wasted fighting for a whole bird would be more than the energy won by settling for half a bird. So we shared the bird and everything else we found during the weeks that we walked north, trapping desert rats and scrub doves, eating grubs and grass and wild rice and the bitter leaves of *neem* trees. We walked north, Jemal seeking relatives while I wanted only to find Nowhere and a world of books, each dreaming of a place of greater safety. By the time we reached Fr. Gianni's mission, we knew there was no place of greater safety.

Fr. Gianni never liked me. My English was already better than his and my skin was dark. With words in my head and darkness in my skin, I was a creature of Satan. When he told us about guilt and damnation and explained that God manifested Himself in the shape of a thin biscuit, I laughed. He was a very funny man, I thought, full of good jokes. Particularly the one about original sin. But he was not telling a joke. He believed it. He had no faith in the messy ways of people muddling through the best they can, making mistakes, and forgiving other people's mistakes the best they can. He was obsessed by blame, tagging everything and everyone 'good' and 'bad,' 'guilty' and 'innocent' to make the world more orderly.

Above all, Fr. Gianni was an *ism* man. His *ism* was Christianism. Like all the *isms* I have seen and read about, Christianism is the choice of men who cannot stand complexity and want to shrink the world to fit their own narrow understanding. That is why I like words and the play we make with them, because they resist the withering regulation of small minds, are wayward and intricate, full of unpredictable patterns, like life itself. There are many ways to tell a story, no single system that everyone must follow, and many ways of reading one, too, because reading is a private recreation that discovers different paths to the heart of each reader. Everyone must find their own crooked way. But the *ism* men are always trying to straighten us out. That was Jemal's problem, too.

He never found his family and naturally wanted no part of a family in which Fr. Gianni was the father, so he hid inside the bigger family of his people's God and the wild hope that one day he would wake up dead in a lovely garden with lovely ladies washing his private parts. We were at that age when the prospect of lovely ladies washing your private parts is enough to recommend any crackpot scheme, no matter how preposterous. Actually, the words he used were *maidens with swelling breasts*. But the mischief was on me when he confessed his secret to me, the only person he could trust in the Christian orphanage, and I put my own construction on it. I told him that if he wanted lovely ladies washing his private parts, he had better be nice to them now, here, on this earth, because there would be no washing of private parts when he was dead. He was not happy. In fact, he was very unhappy. It was all true, he protested, God had told him. No He hadn't, I said, it was the lads from the *madrasa*, and you only had to look at those poor boobies to see they knew even less about lovely ladies washing private parts than we did. Really very, very unhappy. He looked at me like I had just gobbled the entire chicken in a single gulp, leaving him with nothing but a few limp feathers. Mocking his faith, I had betrayed his trust more thoroughly than if I had informed on him. He never forgave me.

Nor did Fr. Gianni forgive the innumerable infractions he detected in my behaviour. They were so many that I became the rebel he required, cultivating any contravention liable to upset him, and making the most of it when I was found out, like the time he caught me drinking the communion wine.

"Why are you drinking the communion wine?" he demanded.

"Because there is no *merissa*," I said.

"You are preferring muddy beer to the blood of our Savior?" he sneered, attempting sarcasm I believe.

"I prefer the spit of a living woman to the blood of a dead man," I said.

Fr. Gianni was nearly sick over his soutane. Fermenting cereals with saliva was clearly not to his taste. He locked me in a hut for two days. But I did not mind. It was the book hut, so I read for two days, holding the books to the light from the crack under the door. I do not know what they did in the mission school during that time. Jemal would not say. He was distracted by God and the lovely ladies.

It was a lovely lady who precipitated my departure from the orphanage. I was thirteen, Mihad was twelve, and we were back in the hut; but instead of books, I was deciphering another stunning composition when the door was flung open with a triumphant shout. At the sight of Mihad's glistening sex, Fr. Gianni staggered backwards, so dazzled that he neglected to stand straight, and stayed crouching as he had been at the doorway. Silhouetted against the sunlight, his hunched profile reminded me of a dog defecating. But I did not tell him. I could see it was not a good moment for a confidence.

He said I was a black devil and would be cast into the pit of hell to suffer eternal torment for my sins. I said he was a white spirit, like we used for cleaning the generator, best kept on the top shelf with the other poisons, and only taken down for dirty jobs. It was all a large mound of camel manure. There is no black, no white, only shades of light and dark, and one day we will all be brown on the outside like we are all brown on the inside, but I was pleased with my retort. Fr. Gianni was not. My departure was swift. I scarcely had time to snatch up a handful of books before he was hustling me out of the compound. There was no opportunity for farewells. Jemal and I had barely spoken since that business about paradise's sanitary arrangements for his private parts, but I would have liked to say goodbye. When next we met, he was a Warrior of God and I was The Story Man.

It all started with the books I had liberated from the store hut. I have stolen many books, most often from the consular libraries because I dislike the way they confine books by classifying them in narrow categories; but none were so important as the half-dozen volumes I had taken from the orphanage, for they were the books that gave me my life. Walking away from Al Asher, I begged food from a family of cowherds. There was little to spare, but they spared it, and in return I gave them a copy of *Great Tales from Shakespeare Made Simple*. Though only the father and the eldest boy could read, and that very approximately, they fell on the book with such keen hunger that I realized I was not the only person with a thirst for stories—and it is hunger and thirst. Reading is alimentary. We devour books and get our teeth into them and lap them up and feast on words if the language is not indigestible. Books are nourishment and, like all nourishment, there is always enough to go round. Only it is not very well distributed. I resolved that I would remedy that.

My ambulant library began with the books I had taken from the mission, but I soon got new volumes from the expatriates. Books are given more gladly than money or food, because the hunger for books is an appetite that implies hope and independence, not despair and dependence. It is good to give something that looks to the future, not the present or the past. Very many times, when white people want to give something to Africa, they give without joy, giving because they feel guilty about what they have now or about what they took long ago, reaching into their pockets, as if they owe a debt that can be paid with money. White people are very guilty people. You only have to look at their literature to see that. The books of Mr. Hawthorne alone have got enough guilt in them to decorate a presidential palace; Mr. Poe has the stuff beating away under the floorboards, Mr. Hardy depicts it seeping through the ceiling, and Mr. Conrad stains entire continents with it; Mr. Stevenson, Mr. Steinbeck, Mr. Styron, they are all always worrying at guilt. Even their radio broadcasts announce that guilt is up, as if it can be measured like water in a well. But giving a book, we get away from guilt and the ghosts it invokes, giving instead something positive to the future, because all the unborn readers that will be are implicit in every book, like an unspoken promise. It is a true gift, untainted by self-interest, a gift that is meant to benefit the recipient more than the donor. In a short time, I had over eighty books, most out on loan, but with a score or so in my pack and more stored in my memory; and when my cotton cloth wore through, an English teacher gave me a canvas rucksack with a metal frame so that I could carry my stock from village to village.

Most of the country people were too poor to pay to borrow books, but in Africa we are used to making a living where there is no money, so each community subscribed to my library by providing me with a cot, food and *merissa*. Later, out of kindness or disquiet, for every African understands the opening lines of *Pride and Prejudice*, a wife would come with the bed, and with the wife a hut, a vegetable garden, and occasionally a goat. There was no permanence about these unions and most of my wives went on to marry other men, but while together we would live as husband and wife. I never fathered any children, though. The stories were my children. I watched them grow, saw them break out and away into other people's heads, and I was glad. That was what I wanted. I wanted people to make stories happen for themselves, like I had learned to do with *Tricycle Tim*.

Since many villagers could not read, I also performed my stories in public, reading aloud, telling from memory when the books were borrowed elsewhere. Reading each story as I traveled, I would tell different parts in different places at different times. Each village heard the story in a different order and no village ever heard the whole story in sequence. Some had to guess why Ahab hated the white whale, others had to work out why the golden doubloon was nailed to the mast, and when people from different villages met at market, they would tell each other what they knew, explaining Queequeg's coffin, the nature of the

Parsee's riddle, or the horror that made Pip mad. It was not as good as reading, but they could piece the story together for themselves and show it back to each other.

To the villagers, I was The Story Man, but the white people called me The Barefoot Librarian. I was never barefoot, but I did not mind the wrong name. It meant something to them, like the roads on their maps. For thirteen years, I walked from village to village. I believe I walked nearly twenty thousand miles. Then the war got big again and once again everything fell apart.

❋ ❋ ❋

Beyond the backwash of the headlights, the distant village is shrouded in darkness. The truck pitches back and forth, bouncing across belts of track, swerving through patches of churned sand, skirting the scars of empty pools, and weaving between the lilac skeletons of dead trees. Our fellow passengers sleep fitfully, jolted in and out of their dreams by the listing of the vehicle. I scan the horizon while Kate presses buttons on the back of her camera, transferring photos from the internal memory. I do not know what she means by this, but I like the words for they could as easily describe reading, which is a transferal from the internal memory to the external, unlocking what has been buried in the book and bringing it to light. It is a kind of archeology, unearthing what has been conserved in the accumulated layers of a narrative.

There is a copy of *Moby Dick* in my shoulder bag, a book in which I discover new treasures with every reading. I always have a book with me, even when I am fetching new stock. It is a necessary companion, like certain beliefs are necessary. I have heard of people who need words so much that they must read the labels on bottles of disinfectants when they sit on the toilet. Here we have few disinfectants, squat instead of sit, and flies would soon displace anyone who settled down to read in a toilet, but I understand that need. I am compelled to read everything. I have even been known to read government decrees pinned to the post office wall. Sometimes, I read trees, spelling an alphabet of my own making among the encrypted letters of the crisscrossing branches.

The truck lurches through an exceptionally deep rut throwing Kate against me. She rights herself promptly, but not before I feel the pressure of her bosoms against my upper arm. I am not mispleased that my country never had the means to make a proper road along this route. They say that small things please small minds, but Kate's bosoms are not such small things and, no matter how petty the pleasure, I feel that this brief collision of bodies brings us closer together in more ways than the mere bumping of flesh against flesh. We are fellow travelers now, the shared mishap and mutual apologies declaring a bond that will last at least for the duration of the journey. Her camera has fallen from her hands and she cannot easily reach it as she steadies herself against the side of the truck, which continues to tilt violently. I retrieve the camera and hand it to her.

"Thank you," she says, checking to see that it is not damaged.

"You are welcome, Miss Kate," I say, and again I see that peculiar look of irritation pass over her face, but she says nothing. "You should put your camera away now," I add. "When the others wake, they will want their photos taken and they are too many for one film."

My people have a passion for pictures of themselves and, since some visitors have had the wit to travel with those cameras they call Polaroid, every foreigner is expected to dispense photographs, like gentlemen callers leaving their cards.

"It doesn't use film," she says, but she does as I suggest, stowing the camera in a large clear plastic bag with a white zipper.

Waiting for the light to come, I gaze across the *qoz* toward the blue hump of the mountain, listening for the welcoming sounds of the waking village. Mine has been a footloose life, but I know the pleasures of sedentary living well enough to love the music of community. At night, the day fades to a declining harmony, the crackle of fires, the murmur of voices, snatches of laughter or chanted song, the cooing of doves, a goat or donkey giving voice to the intolerable fatigue of being, all gradually growing fainter until the only sound is the hum of cicadas and the intermittent barking of a dog. Come morning, the composition is played in reverse, cocks crowing against the dark, dogs, donkeys and goats stirring themselves, men hawking and spitting, women rousing unwilling children and going about their household tasks, pouring water into tin basins, clanking pans, sparking fires, the chorus growing to greet the rising sun . . . it is an orchestra of life blowing and banging and plucking and sawing its way into the rhythms of the day.

Though still sat upright, the small of her back braced against the exposed upper slats of the truck bed, Kate has let her head drop and closed her eyes, taking advantage of a smoother stretch of ground to sleep for a few moments. She still sways slightly and several times I think she is about to topple toward me, so that I lean forward, prepared to prevent her falling. On each occasion though, she catches herself, without waking it would seem, and sits straight again. I watch her for a while, still marveling that a white woman should travel alone in this place at this time, wondering whether what she told us last night is true or, being true, whether it does not conceal some other purpose. Hardly anybody stays here who does not have to, and those that do are motivated by degrees of greed or idealism that would seem implausible had one not read a little history detailing the many elaborate lunacies of human behavior. Kate stirs, so I turn aside, not wanting her to wake and find me staring at her. In the same way that silence makes them uneasy, unmediated curiosity is something white people do not accept well. Like life's other vital functions, they feel it is an unruly beast that must be indulged at one remove or inhibited by a counterfeit diffidence, as if other people and their doings are not endlessly fascinating.

There is still no sign of the village, but a thin rime of light smears itself along the horizon, then steals across the shallow undulations of the *qoz*, discovering the bleached bones of a camel, the scurrying, flitting, hopping progress of hectic gerbils, panicky mice, tiny scrub doves, and thumb-sized sparrows, and in the distance a large black and white bird circling against the whitening mountain. Within an hour, the light will be so bright that the mountain will look small, as if squashed by the weight of the sun, and the *qoz* will have been smoothed into an apparently seamless carpet of flat scrub. It is not true, this trick of the light. The mountain is large and full of complex folds, and even the lowlands are laced with a web of *wadis,* like a shattered labyrinth scattered across the plain. It is these seasonal watercourses that bring life to the *qoz*, draining rainfall from the mountain and distributing it about a riverless landscape where human settlement depends on bore holes. The arid land looks bleak and empty, but it is full of life, both wild and domestic, and—in the gaps between what is native—I have sown yet more life, embellishing the terrain with characters and stories culled from books. I am a grower of stories, I farm them as I would millet, a way of surviving in the world, assuaging hunger and confirming the future.

There are nearly forty of us squeezed onto the back of the truck, so tight together that the white sacks of sorghum are almost hidden. One by one, the others wake, turning toward the mountain and the village, looking forward to the *chai* shack and the peck of fire, the wood fed tip first into the small flame to eke out the warmth. *Chai* and *kisra* will be served, and Kate will be called upon to repeat last night's litany, replying to the standard interrogation: Where are you from? What are you doing? Where are you going? What is your religion? Are you married? She will be plied with food and drink that she can probably better afford than her hosts, then the questioning will begin again in more painstaking detail, piecing together a sketchy picture of far-off people in far-off places employed in far-out practices. Once more, she will reply with the deft fluency of one who has been quizzed many times before, ducking the question of God, but admitting that she has no husband. Like the other passengers last night, the people in the *chai* shack will be saddened by her single status, puzzled by the talk of gender studies and traditional societies, and mystified as to why she should write about such things to become a doctor.

That is how it should be, standard questions breaking the night's fast, but there are no questions asked when we reach the village. Everyone understands what has happened. The *chai* shack is no longer there. A dented pan, some charred shards of glass, a blackened back-broke bench, and a few sheaves of scorched grass are all that remains. Accidents are not uncommon. Thatch burns easily and, even when a fire is tended carefully, the bottles used as chimneys can catch the sun's rays and ignite the roof. But this fire is no accident. Behind the burned *quitiyya,* the cluster of huts that constituted the main village have also been destroyed. The walls of the mud buildings have caved in, everything that would not burn and could not be taken has been smashed, and there is a terrible stillness overlaid with a faint humming sound.

A woman near the front of the truck starts moaning. The sound is not loud, but comes from deep in her throat, like something leaking from a badly sealed container. She taps her chest with the knuckles of her clenched fist, rocking slowly back and forth. The driver and cab passengers descend, but do not move far from the open doors, as if fearing others will take their place. The rest of us drop lightly from the back of the truck, unwilling to draw attention to ourselves by any unnecessary noise, until only the woman and three children remain. There is nothing to do, nothing to see that we want to see, yet one by one we walk into the village that is no more.

The humming becomes a buzz as an angry black cloud of flies rises from the ground, uncovering the corpses of a dozen people and a score of animals. Many of the villagers are missing, but they will not have escaped. Some will have been taken by the raiders along with the livestock, others may have been shut in the huts to burn, but most will have been driven into the *qoz*, away from the wells, and left to survive as best they can, perhaps to reach a camp, but no more, no better than that, for the government ensures the help they need cannot reach them.

Who has been here? The Warriors of God? The People's Popular Liberation Army? The Revolutionary Spirit Front? The ADF, the FNI, the JIP, the PLM? IPLM? MIC? PLC? There are dozens of these groups, some so few in number that they are little more than extended families, others amounting to small armies. Some are politicals, some believe they are the instruments of God, others are just bandits, but it hardly matters who has done this work, for they are all the same, all a part of the alphabet soup of suffering, an alphabet that is often better taught in this world than the proper literacy of language and words and the sentiments they bring to life.

I am standing beside the body of a man. His eyes have been plucked out, his ears cut off, and he has been castrated, the bloody holes parodying the purpose of eyes, ears and genitalia with a ghastly, dilapidated emptiness. Another body has had the hands and feet hacked off. A dead child lies on his side, curled in an attitude of sleep, except one arm is flung back, casually, as if reaching for something behind him, but stretched too far for comfort. His face has been smashed and the bone at the back of the skull is flat where it has been clubbed by a rifle butt. Some of the adults have been more fortunate, killed by a bullet through the back of the head. I do not like to think of what lies in the collapsed huts, but there is a sweet smell of cooked meat.

A woman appears. She is wearing no clothes and has clearly been crawling across the ground though she is standing now. Her front is crusted with dirt and dust, stuck to her skin by the blood shed from the wounds where her breasts used to be. It is the lips that disturb me most, though, the lips above and the lips below. Both have been cut, probably before she was raped, so that her mouth is a naked grimace and the insides of her thighs are sticky with gore. The men with guns and horses always go for the lips, the lips that are the most tender part of humanity and the most expressive, through which we speak to one another in different languages of love and learning. It is the lips below that make them most angry because the lips of a woman's sex tell a language no man can talk. That is something that always provokes men with a liking for violence, an articulacy that they cannot ape.

I am a misfit, of course. Ever since Mihad's mauve lips scared Fr. Gianni so badly, I have loved to look at that part of a woman when I lie with her, yet my people are shy of their reproductive organs. In many villages, it is considered a misfortune for a woman to see her husband's member and couplings are done in the dark, not with shame, but encumbered by a burdensome modesty. Worse, even before the war grew large again, there were places where women were mutilated because that was the time-honored custom. And I have seen the victims of war often enough, those women caught foraging for wood around the camps, the young girls discarded after being used, thrown away more casually than anyone here would dispose of something so useful as a plastic bag. I should be used to it. But I am not. There is something about this cutting of the lips before the raping, something that goes beyond an act of war, something that makes me wish Jemal would do what he has long promised to do and kill me because this maimed, maiming world is not one in which I wish to live. Even books cannot make sense of it.

The woman staggers towards us, drawn by the truck and the thought of people and help and safety, as if such things can still exist for her. Nobody reacts because none of us know how to respond to this living unsexed thing that no longer looks quite human. Then I see a movement off to my left. It is Kate. She is walking toward the woman, holding her hands out, as if carrying a tray, or greeting a guest. But there is no offering in her hands, no welcome on her face, just the wooden anguish that we all feel when we see how very wrong the world can be and know that there is nothing we can do about it. That is what I think at the time, though later I learn Kate does believe there is something she can do about it.

The woman stumbles, steps left, as if to evade the meeting, then tilts forward and falls into Kate's arms. Kate catches her, bends to keep her from hitting the ground, then rapidly kneels, lowering the woman into her lap. The whole maneuver is done with such delicacy, such lightness, even grace, that I am again, despite the situation, moved by the strangeness of Kate, for it is as if, in seeing the worst of what people can do, we are also seeing the best, the simple compassion that can take a broken bleeding thing that men have done their utmost to degrade, and find in that thing a fellow being in need of human comfort.

Kate catching this pitiful fractured creature breaks whatever spell it is that has stilled the rest of us and several women rush to her aid, one elderly lady unwinding her own *tobe* to cover the woman's nakedness. Two men return to the truck to fetch the shovels used for digging free the wheels and drive shaft when the vehicle is stuck in sand, while others gather rocks to pile on the shallow graves. It serves no purpose. There is no covering what has happened to this woman, no burying what has happened to this village, but the activity helps; it makes us think we are doing something, can do something.

Then I see something else I do not understand. Kate has extracted herself from the deconstructed woman. Her dress is smeared with the woman's blood. She is moving swiftly between the bodies before the men come to take them away. Fortunately, nobody else sees what she is doing, or seeing, they do not believe. It would not make her popular. Even I am shocked. She is taking photographs.

❂ ❂ ❂

We are all somehow dreadfully cracked about the head and sadly need mending.
There is no folly of the beasts of the earth which is not infinitely outdone by the madness of men.

These are the words of Mr. Melville. I admire Mr. Melville very much, but I sometimes wonder whether his estimation of humankind is correct. Are we merely cracked? Can we be mended? Or are we made like this, born with an inestimable capacity for insanity? On occasion, it even occurs to me that Fr. Gianni's jest about original sin might not have been so deranged after all. When I look at all the mad, bad, misguided things we do, I sometimes think the world is merely a very large prison, that one day long ago all the other planets got together to discuss what to do with their killers and criminals, and decided the killers and criminals should be set aside in one place, and that place is the Earth, and we are the progeny of killers and criminals, and all the other planets are watching, waiting for us to finally do away with ourselves. Even we, mad, bad, and misguided as we are, foresee our fate, broadcasting our imminent demise on the radio. On the BBC World Service, they say "that is the end of the world news" and they are right, everyday is the end of the world news. The Warriors of God would like that phrase if they knew any word play. But they don't. They know no play at all. For them, everything is fixed and permanent, everything to its place. At present, their place is some way off to the south of us. They are riding across the *qoz*, shadowing the painfully slow progress of the truck.

The woman died of her wounds before we left and was buried with her kin. It was a mercy, for the violent movement of the truck would only have caused her greater suffering and would likely have killed her anyway. So our journey continues, around the mountain toward Al Asher, the crossroads and the well of books, our departure from the dead village conducted in silence save for the grinding gears of the truck, the stillness of the air broken only by isolated dust-devils twisting across the desert, harbingers of a *haboob*. The curtain of sand is not visible yet, nor can we feel the wind, but it will come, and maybe at this season it will bring rain with it, in which case we will not make Al Asher tonight. But that is the least of our worries.

When we first see the Warriors of God, they are nothing more than a flat plume of dust in the distance. They might even be part of the *haboob*, for no vehicle or horseman can be distinguished, only a thin band of sand kicked up by hooves and wheels. Some among us pretend it is part of the storm, a natural happening from which we can shelter, but at heart we all know that there is no hiding from the winds of history, not here, not now, not in this place and time.

"Why?" asks Kate, speaking quietly, almost to herself, though in fact the word is directed at me. She is not questioning the winds of history, nor Mr. Melville's notion that we are all dreadfully cracked about the head, but why the horsemen are tracking us.

"They are bandits, Miss Kate."

"My name is Kate," she says, "just Kate."

"Yes, Miss Kate."

She looks irritated, but does not protest. If she wishes to understand my country, which is what she told her questioners last night, she must learn to live with courtesy. Etiquette, rank, and codes of behavior are as important here as they are in the books of Miss Austen. I sometimes suspect that nowadays we Africans understand Miss Austen's concerns better than her compatriots do.

"But I thought they were paid by the government."

"They are. $116 a month. And a gun and a horse. But their salaries come from what they take. If they do not steal, they do not get paid. So they learn the habits of banditry, just as the rebels do. Finders keepers, you say, I think."

It is a perfect war. It pays for itself.

Kate takes a notebook from the clear plastic bag in which she stored her camera and dutifully writes down the figure of $116, another fact for her collection, a fact to go with the photos. I still do not understand why she took the photos. True, it is not a prohibition like with a beast due for slaughter, but who wants to see photos of dead bodies? It is simply another state of being, different in kind from living, but not to be preserved in pictures. Pictures, in any case, preserve nothing because they do not engage the imagination like words. Only the imagination can make things live again, and even then it is no more than a sleight of mind.

The column to the south has changed course and is beginning to bear down on the truck. The Landcruiser leading the horsemen is clearly visible now, confirming that these are the Warriors of God rather than another group of men with guns and horses. Our driver accelerates until the truck is no longer bucking but slews from side to side. He cannot outrun the Landcruiser and at this speed a tire is almost bound to burst, the ancient patched tubes will not take such punishment for long, but I understand that he has to try. There is nothing else to do.

The Warriors of God do not seem concerned by our attempt to get away. The horses continue to trot, the Landcruiser maintains a steady speed, and one might even suppose they are ready to let us go, were it not for the fact that the column reorients itself to narrow the angle of interception. Our paths will converge later, but they will converge, of that there is no question.

The why is still there, though; not the why of 'Why us?' There could be any number of reasons for that or none at all, but why are we so dreadfully cracked about the head? Maybe we are made that way, but perhaps it is also because we tell ourselves the wrong stories, stories of safety and escape and heroes capable of controlling some small part of their destiny, when in truth there is no escape, only a tissue of passing moments when we are at peace with ourselves and one another. Still, we pretend, cultivating illusions of security, traveling together on the back of a truck because we believe numbers will keep us safe, taking refuge in small fictions, peopling our lives with dream companions, riding in armed gangs because the power over other people's lives makes us think we are in control of our own. They are necessary beliefs, minor deceits without which we would not be able to make it through the day.

We reach a relatively firm stretch of ground with few rocks and the truck picks up speed again, rattling along at forty miles an hour so that the passengers have to cling onto the slats and sacks to avoid being flung overboard, like poor Pip tossed from Mr. Stubbs' boat. The horses have also increased their speed, not quite galloping, but cantering fast enough to ensure the truck will not escape. There is no pretending it is just chance, that they simply happen to be heading in the same direction as us. We are their target, they are less than half-a-mile distant from us, and the Landcruiser is already pulling ahead.

Several of those on the back of the truck are lying flat, hiding their faces, others have their eyes shut; only Kate and the children appear to be looking directly at the Warriors of God. I have my hand in my shoulder bag. I am holding *Moby Dick*, murmuring to myself a consoling song of the characters that have walked with me through the years: Mr. Micawber, Pudd'nhead Wilson, Miss Marple, Oliver Twist, Squire Allworthy, Captain Wentworth, David Copperfield, Billy Budd, Natty Bumppo, Hercule Poirot, Louisa Musgrove, Maggie Tulliver, Silas Marner, Martin Eden, Adam Bede, Gabriel Oak. . . . There is no hope in this invocation, but it is comforting to conjure good companions, just as the horsemen hope to save themselves by calling upon their God, and the government requires enemies and conspiracies lest they feel alone and abandoned in this world. We all have phantoms that help keep us going.

Now the moment has come. No book is going to make any difference here, no nonsense is proof against the designs of these men. They ride well, have lived long in the saddle, and on a whim it seems they turn their horses toward the truck, the Landcruiser swings around to cut us off, and there is a crackling as the first shots are fired. Everyone lies flat, even Kate, as the truck crashes on, a great crippled beast making a last bid for survival. We bounce through a shallow *wadi* and there is a shriek as a man at the back is shaken loose and thrown from the truck, disappearing in the cloud kicked up by our wheels. I raise my head to see where he has fallen, but the trail of sand is so thick that there is no sign of him. Beyond, the sky is red and orange and I can feel the hot wind on my face, strong despite the speed of the retreating truck. The storm is coming.

The horsemen continue to ride hard, bracing their rifles against their shoulders and loosing off sporadic one-handed potshots, declarations of intent rather than a properly directed attack. A hole appears in the sack in front of my face and there is a curiously soft sound as another bullet skids across the roof of the cab leaving a dark mark on the metal. The horsemen's clothes billow back and forth, filled with air from their onward motion, then puffed into swollen chests by the approaching storm. Travelers dread the *haboob*, for it can suck the life from a truck's engine or bury the axles so deep that it will take an entire day to disinter them; but this time it is welcome for there is a hope that it might help some of us get away.

There is a different report among the gunshots, a sound closer and sharper, then the truck twists, spins and tips, flinging the passengers from the top. I am not the first to find my feet. Already, other men are running and Kate has disappeared. People are lying on the ground, knocked unconscious or worse, and one woman is crawling, her left leg bent sideways at the knee. Several sacks of *dura* have fallen overboard and burst, but the bulk of the cargo was so tightly packed that it is still inside the truck, which is on its side, the cab door open, like the wing of a clumsy bird that has crashed in flight. The Landcruiser has pulled up fifty paces ahead of the wreck. The horsemen are closing in. The passengers, so numerous and crowded on the truck, seem pitifully few now that they are scattering across the plain, but there are still more of them than horsemen, obliging the Warriors of God to weave back and forth in pursuit of the fleeing figures, which cannot please men who favor straight lines in everything they do. They look blurred, veiled in some gauzy material, making me think I am concussed. Then I feel the grit on my skin, my breathing becomes more labored, and I realize the *haboob* has begun.

My shoulder bag is on the ground. Stupidly, I bend to pick it up, as if a book, a cake of *sim-sim*, and a handful of groundnuts can be any use here. As I straighten, something hard hits me on the shoulder, knocking me sideways. I turn to face my assailant, who is holding an old sword. He handles it awkwardly, for he has lost the skills of his fathers, or if not lost them, learned new methods of expressing old talents, and has hit me with the flat of the blade rather than the cutting edge. The gunfire is less regular now, the Warriors of God are brandishing blades, short and long, saving their ammunition for more valuable prey. The man in front of me draws back his sword to strike again. I lash out with my shoulder bag, catching him in the face with the weight of *Moby Dick*. The blow does no damage, but it distracts him long enough, makes him step back, and I leap at him, shoving him hard in the chest. The man topples backwards and the upraised sword sticks in the ground behind him as we fall so that he cuts himself with his own blade. The wound is not deep, certainly not fatal, but he cries out and rolls aside, clutching his neck.

Standing, I look around me, trying to see which way to run, but the sandstorm is denser now and only the shadowy figures within a few feet of me are identifiable as passengers or Warriors of God. My bag has fallen to one side in the struggle and, again without thinking, I bend to pick it up, slinging it over my shoulder, and again this heedlessness is the saving of me.

In front of the truck, a Warrior of God has grabbed one of the children by the neck, holding him with his left hand while the right gropes for the dagger strapped to his upper arm. Big shoulders, strong arms. This is not a boast. It is just what you get from carrying books around all your life. The rock catches the man on the side of the head and he crumples to the ground. "Run!" I shout. "Run! Run! Run!" The boy looks at me as if I am mad. Maybe I am, for there's nowhere to run except into the thickening storm, but he concludes it is best to run, even if there is nowhere to go.

Then I hear another loud noise and I am thrown forward and I know that I have been shot though there is no pain. I stand up, turn around. Jemal is staring at me in disbelief, a pistol in his hand. Several of his men are nearby and the horror on their faces is such that in any other circumstances I would laugh out loud for the love of it. 'Twas brillig, and the slithy toves did gyre and gimble in the wabe. This is not what these men have come to expect. They have their guns, they have their horses, they have their amulets, their shouted charms, their God with His beautiful names, they have their government's dispensation to kill, they have power and are pleased with it, for they are supreme and nobody can stand in their way. With such an armory at their disposal, they are not accustomed to people who will not lay down and die when that is what is required of them. I do not yet understand what has happened. I know I have been shot, not well perhaps, but close enough for killing or, at the very least, crippling. I can feel a dull ache like a deep bruise below my shoulder blade and along the side of my ribs. I know I should not be standing like this, that I should be dead just as they want and expect me to be. But I am not. I am standing, living proof that the Warriors of God are not invincible.

Then the rain comes. At first it is nothing more than a freshening of the swirling sand, but when the real violence declares itself the sand becomes dense and damp, and before long it is raining mud, thick sheets of blinding mud eclipsing the already obscure figures so that anybody more than an arm's stretch away can barely be seen.

Jemal realizes he is about to lose sight of me and that, if I disappear, his men will be haunted by the phantom of someone they cannot kill, a man blessed with the invulnerability they crave for themselves, a man whose very existence will make them doubt, and they are not men to tolerate doubt. Jemal fires again, but I am back on the ground, rolling sideways despite the pain in my shoulder, putting the carcass of the truck between myself and the gun. Jemal fires wildly, repeatedly, but the bullets find no more flesh, or none of mine, at least.

Up on my feet again, I start to run as fast I can through the falling mud. A horseman looms out of the darkness, but I am so buoyed by survival that I simply reach out and pluck him from the saddle, disposing of him on the ground, almost casually, and keep running, running into the darkness because in this world that is all you can do.

◙　◙　◙

Life is a labyrinth, but we read it in different ways. For men like the Warriors of God it is a labyrinth because they believe there is only one way to the heart of things and anyone taking the wrong path will be lost. For me it is a labyrinth like a good detective tale is a labyrinth, full of false trails and digressions that can be as engaging as the correct interpretation, a story in which there is no shame in going back and checking turnings you may have missed, because the journey is more important than what lies at the end. Sometimes, though, there are more compelling reasons for turning back. Sometimes, it is a matter of survival.

The storm has abated and I am returning to the truck, following the winding *wadi* and low-lying ground so that I will not be seen from a distance. The groundnuts and *sim-sim* will not sustain me in this place, still less my *Moby*

Dick with the neat hole drilled through it by Jemal's bullet, so I must go back to the truck to look for food. The wound in my back hurts now, but I do not believe it is deep. I cannot see it, but I can feel the furrow below my shoulder blade, fringed with untidy lips of torn flesh.

The Warriors of God have gone. Several sacks of *dura* have been taken, presumably transferred to the Land-cruiser, but most of the load is still lodged in the bed of the truck under a blanket of sand. Off to the right, there is a body, near the tailgate two more sand-mantled heaps that might be corpses, and a cluster of vultures are tracing patient circles above some unseen attraction to the south. Behind the cobwebbed glass of the cab's broken wind-screen, I can make out the slumped bodies of the driver and one of his passengers. Only when I am within a few paces of the truck does the figure appear from behind it, a standing figure, still living, still walking.

Clothes torn, caked in mud, face blackened by grime, hair blasted into odd spikes by the wind and dirt, it looks more like a golem than anything human, and judging by the way it stops and stares, my own aspect is no more promising. A couple of unhandily made dolls, Kate and I gawk at one another, each as alarmed as the other. In the circumstances, this is not a place where one spontaneously welcomes casual encounters. The Warriors of God cannot be far away and I have no desire whatsoever to bump into them. They need me dead now like they never needed me dead before, every step I take giving the lie to their perfect invincibility. It is a lesson they need to learn because, as Mr. Melville says, any human thing supposed to be complete, must for that very reason infallibly be faulty. But they are not of a kind to learn lessons. They are more inclined to teach lessons.

"You are hurt?" says Kate, gesturing at a black stain of blood that has spread across the gusset of my waistcoat. Before I have time to reply, she walks over, briskly solicitous, bending to inspect the torn cloth. "May I?" she says, reaching toward the ragged fabric. She may. A woman's touch, no matter how neutral, is always therapeutic. After a moment, she says: "I can't see it properly. You must take your top off." I hesitate, then pull the waistcoat and long shirt over my head. She is no medical doctor, but her touch is light, businesslike. Even so, it stings when her fingers brush across the wound and I can't quite suppress a hissing intake of breath. "I'm sorry. You don't have any antiseptic, do you?" I laugh at her question. She knows full well that this is not an antiseptic place. "We must at least wash it," she says.

"We must at least leave as soon as we can," I counter, putting my clothes back on and picking up my shoulder bag, tired of this little performance and reminded by the pain of how dangerous our situation is. The waterskins on the cab of the truck have burst, but the one hanging from the tailgate is whole, and only a small quantity has evaporated, for the mud and sand have formed an additional carapace sealing shut the pores. I pull it free of the wreckage and tie the fore and hind legs together to form a sling. "You had a backpack?"

"It's gone. They've taken all the bags."

Not quite. Under the driver's seat I find a hold-all with a shoulder strap. It is large enough for perhaps a fifth, maybe less, of a sack of *dura*, which is not enough, but will do. There is a bag of okra, too, three loaves of bread, some dry beans, a packet of sesame seeds, some salt, a battered tin cup, a pan and a plastic bucket. I take everything.

"OK, let's go, please."

"Wait. My camera. I came back to find my camera."

"Your camera?" For the first time, I am annoyed by this woman I hardly know, but who I have admired since I saw her standing in the alley, facing down the Warriors of God. No, not 'annoyed.' Say it for what it is. I am angry, anxiety conspiring with the memory of what happened in the village and the suspicion that she has dissembled her purpose here, so that this simple statement seems like a gross impertinence. "You think this is a time for snapshots? Or do you want to take more pictures of dead bodies?"

Her face hardens and I can see something of the mulish defiance with which she treated the Warriors of God, only this time I am its object. It is not an agreeable experience. I have never yet met a woman I did not wish to please, but I would most particularly not want to excite the enmity of a woman like this. Though they are often treated in ways that make foreigners think of them as mere victims, there are many strong and admirably independent women in my country. It is their very strength and independence that provokes the mistreatment. But rarely have I encountered one quite so unyielding. The slight apprehension she inspires in me notwithstanding, I am still more than a little irritated

"Somebody has to," she says.

For a moment, I consider leaving her behind, because books have taught me that self-preservation is an option, too, and I know that I would have a better chance of survival on my own. They have not, however, wholly liberated me from the laws of hospitality. Even now, when so many people have been driven away from community or actively seek to destroy it, a stranger can still claim certain rights.

We look for her camera. I fully expect it to be in the hands of a Warrior of God (what, I wonder, would they make of the pictures she took of their handiwork?), but in fact we find the clear plastic bag some thirty yards behind the wreck, trampled into the sand. The camera and her cell phone have been smashed, but the notebook is still intact and Kate seems relieved. She takes something from inside the broken camera and tosses aside the shell.

"The memory card," she explains, seeing my quizzical glance. It makes no more sense than the talk of an internal memory and is less pleasing, for I do not believe memories are extracted so easily. Some little work is required, some act of the imagination. She slips her so-called memory card between the pages of her notebook, replaces it in the plastic bag, and tucks the package in a pocket hidden inside her dress.

"Can we leave now?" I ask.

Kate looks at me long and hard. Even I am a little surprised at how testy my words sound. It is not the tone I would have used when the accidental pressure of her bosoms made me think we had become fellow travelers. I had thought my recent exasperation had abated somewhat during the search for the camera. But I am frightened now, more frightened by the thought of the Warriors of God returning and finding us here than I was when they were actually attacking the truck. I want to leave this place as soon as possible. She, meanwhile, watches me, apparently scared of nothing, perhaps wondering as I had done whether it would not be wiser or, at least, less complicated, simply to walk away on her own. It is only when she picks up the bucket, leaving the hold-all for me, that I understand she has made her decision, that she will walk with me and share the load of our provisions.

❧ ❧ ❧

It is dark and chill. Foolishly, I did not think to look for the thin blankets we had used the night before, so the cold creeps through our bodies like a slow poison. We are camping in a *wadi*, have eaten bread, groundnuts and *simsim*, not daring to light a fire, when she asks me where we are going. In truth, I do not know. Away was all that mattered. If I have anywhere to go, it is, as planned, to the well of books, but after what has happened I do not believe I can take the books back to Anahud, even to the camps . . .

perhaps especially to the camps. The Warriors of God will not want me, the man they failed to kill, telling the people they have displaced that they are not all powerful. It is bad enough that I have shown that to themselves.

"You must take me to Al Asher," she says, "I have to get to Al Asher."

The 'must' displeases me. In our short acquaintance, she has already used the word more than I would consider normal. It was one of the English words that Fr. Gianni really understood. Along with *mustn't* and *can't* and *should* and *have to* and *ought*. He was very keen on the subtleties of auxiliary verbs, even if the rest of his vocabulary was limited to sets of simple antonyms with no shading in between. But Kate does not notice my displeasure, she is too set upon her goal, which is the way of white people. In their books, they always want to get somewhere, as if they believe that when they reach a destination they will have resolved everything, when in fact all it means is that they are somewhere else and the life they wanted to leave behind continues in a different place.

"The way is too dangerous now. The Warriors of God will be looking for us."

"But you don't understand. I have to get there. I'll go on my own if I have to. Is it in walking distance?"

"Everywhere is in walking distance if you take the time."

It is the sort of reply I practiced on Fr. Gianni and has much the same impact on Kate as it would have had on him.

"I want a straight answer," she says. "I haven't got time for games."

I could give her a Gianni answer to that, too.

"If you went across the plain on foot, it would take four or five days. But you will never arrive. The . . ."

"Warriors of God, I know."

"They will be looking for us."

"And it is because of them that I must reach Al Asher. Is there another way?"

"The mountain will be safer. Might be safer. But I do not know how long that will take. Days, maybe a week, maybe more."

"Will you show me the way?" she asks.

"I do not know the way, not properly."

"I will go on my own then."

"I will show you the way," I say. In books, I believe this is what they call noblesse oblige. In truth, it is, in another phrase I have read and which I like very much, a bloody nuisance. I am beginning to think this determined young lady is more trouble than she is worth. Worse, I do not even know what she is determined on apart from a destination. But I have nowhere else to go and, if we find the way, the well of books is also on the far side of the mountain. I will, at least, have more to read than a copy of *Moby Dick* with a bullet hole through the middle.

❄ ❄ ❄

At the foot of the mountain the run-off has formed many *wadis*, even small valleys; but out on the plain there are places where the channels have been blocked by drifting sand, forcing us to walk without cover, silhouetted against the horizon. It is in just such a place that we first see the horsemen.

Kate is ahead of me. It is early morning, the sun still too low to dispel the chill of the night. She has her head down, is not properly awake, hardly looks where she is walking, but I am watchful, resisting the temptation to pass the time contemplating her calves and glimpsing the dimpled crease behind each knee. I have other things to watch, less beguiling perhaps, but no less vital. A landscape is like a book, each a kind of code that the traveler must decipher.

The *qoz* looks flat, but to the east, a pale shadow betrays a shallow depression, while behind us a thin trimming of coarse grass lines the lip of the otherwise invisible *wadi* we have just left. Beyond the depression, a faint rippling is serrated by the sun, suggesting the furrows of a watershed where the wind and rain have scoured an unseen slope. I am watching this rise, knowing it is dangerous, when a tiny glint flashes across the rim, as if a rock laced with a bright mineral has caught the sun's rays.

"Hssst!"

Kate is too slow. She is still turning when I shove her in the small of the back knocking her to the ground.

"What the . . . what are you . . ."

She twists around, trying to stand. I scramble on top of her, pushing her down. She struggles, thinking I am attacking her. I press an arm across her chest, a hand over her mouth, holding her still. She can neither move nor speak, pinioned as she is by book muscle, but still she squirms, trying to free herself. We are so close that our bodies are melded like the bodies of lovers, but I take no pleasure from the intimacy because we are brought together by danger not desire.

I gesture with my head toward the east. Something in my eyes persuades her the threat does not come from this strange man lying on top of her. Her glance slides sideways as the barrel of the gun that had glinted in the sun reveals itself and we see the first horseman. The butt of the gun is propped against his hip, the stock cradled in his right hand, more from habit than readiness, I hope. Two more horsemen appear behind him. I cannot tell if they are Warriors of God, but it is no time for introductions. Whoever they are, they are looking for someone. They pause on the rise, turn to scan the *qoz*, then ride toward us.

Kate has stopped struggling, is staring at the approaching horsemen. She does not notice at first that I have slipped off her and am palming sandy earth over her legs. We are both so filthy that we are already the color of the earth, but they will spot us if they continue on their present course. When she sees what I am doing, she understands immediately, and starts scraping the earth over herself.

"You?" she mouths, indicating that I must hide as well. But my dark skin is an asset and I want her completely covered because there are still pale patches showing through the grime. When even her hands and most of her face are camouflaged, I flatten myself behind her, bury the bright plastic bucket and the bags, and hurriedly scrape a trench along the length of her body. The horsemen are perhaps a quarter-of-a-mile away now, moving slowly, still coming toward us, watching all the while. There is no time to dig deeper. I slide into my hastily excavated grave and flip a thin layer of dirt over myself. I cannot cover everything, but enough I hope.

The sun has risen and the sand begins to warm as we lie there, like a couple of apprentice cadavers, which is pretty much what Jemal and his men think I am. I have never done this before, never inhumed myself, but the sensation is familiar, for it is what I have been doing my whole life long with reading, burying myself in books so that I will be invisible to the outside world and the outside world will be invisible to me. Inter yourself one way or another and you will feel safe, however illusory that safety might be.

The horsemen are not readers. If they were readers, they would know that you must pay attention to small details. But they are not schooled in the ways of decryption. You don't need clues when you think you understand everything. I hear them pass, conversing in dull, bored voices, perhaps fifty feet from where we are lying, barely daring to breathe. When they have ridden a little further, I raise my head, leaving most of my body covered, and turn to watch. It is imprudent, nothing more than curiosity, but curiosity is a defect of most readers. We all want to know what is happening behind this cover, over that hill, within those walls, we are hungry for stories of all sorts. The men sit straight on their horses, their heads upright, still scanning the horizon. They have their eyes fixed on distant prospects and are blind to what surrounds them. Sometimes, it is as well that certain men do not see too clearly.

When they are nearly out of sight, I tell Kate she can sit up, but not stand. She shakes the sand off, emerging from the earth, as if I have conjured her up from the underworld with my imagination. Had it not been too risky, I would have liked us both to have risen out of the ground while the Warriors of God were nearby. Had I been on my own, I might have done so. It would almost be worth dying just to see the alarm on their faces in the first moments before understanding triggered anger.

"I'm sorry," she says. "For struggling, I mean. I hadn't seen them. Were they looking for us, do you think?"

"I do not know, but I do not want to wait and find out. If they were, there will be others, too. You see why the *qoz* is dangerous? In the mountain at least we will have more places to hide."

"And on the other side?"

She is right. Al Asher is at least a day's walk after the mountain. The crossroads is nearer and is occasionally patrolled by troops of the peacekeeping corps—a great joke in the camps, I can assure you. Otherwise there will be the same dangerous terrain, the same deceptive flatness, and the same risks of being seen. But we are not there yet.

❖   ❖   ❖

All day, we walk north toward the mountain. It is the coolest time of year and the nights are cold, but the heat of the midday sun can still overpower people who are not used to it. Kate does not complain, she is more Agnes Wickfield than Mrs. Gummidge, but I can see she is tired.

"Miss Kate, we must rest."

If we reach the mountain, she will need all her energy. I have not crossed the high ground before, but I know there are many wild places there, places as harsh and barren as any in the desert.

"Kate, just Kate," she says, still irritated it would seem by my commonplace courtesy.

"OK, Just Kate, we must rest."

"Very funny. Why do you call me that? 'Miss Kate.' It sounds so, I don't know, servile . . . so old-fashioned."

"Why are you troubled by servility? Your writers always make it dishonest or embarrassing. But there is no shame in serving other people."

"It is embarrassing. There is a history, you know. I didn't come here to be treated like some old colonial."

"Why did you come here then?" I ask, and her face changes again, becomes more wary, as if she fears her tetchiness will betray her into revealing something best kept secret.

"I told you. My doctorate about how women coped with the famine."

I do not trust her in this. In everything else she is forthright and candid, but there is something devious about her professed motives. Yet looking into her dark green eyes, I see no deceit. They do not appear to blink nor slide away from my gaze. They are honest eyes in an honest face.

"That is why you take photos of dead people?"

"That is something else," she says, tight-lipped.

"We must stop, anyway."

We shelter below a *neem* tree in a hollow where rainwater gathers. There is no standing water, but the depression is damp from the storm, and it is a good spot to pass the hottest hours of the day. Kate sleeps briefly while I pick leaves and a small crust of bark from the tree, grinding them between stones then mixing them with a little water in the tin cup, which I wedge inside the small pocket of my waistcoat. A decoction or an oil would be better, but in the circumstances, I will have to make do with this crude paste. Later, we walk for another two hours, no more, since we must not exhaust ourselves on this, the easiest if most dangerous leg of our journey.

The *wadis* are deeper now that we are nearing the mountain, but even in the lee of the riverbed where we settle for the night, I still do not dare light a fire. In the highlands, we can make *kisra*, cook the okra and beans. This evening, we finish the bread, eat more groundnuts and *sim-sim*.

Afterwards, I place the tin cup in front of me and strip to the waist. I cannot see my wound clearly, but when Kate notices what I am trying to do, she offers to help. This is not an antiseptic place, but we have our ways, just as it is not a safe place, but we carry on living, not a happy place, but we keep laughing. Life goes on, even when you are surrounded by the end of the world news.

Something about the intimacy of the moment loosens Kate's tongue. While she gently works the paste into the wound, she talks, and her words help numb the pain. With little prompting, she tells me about her life, tells me tales of a weak mother absorbed in self-pity, of an absent father guiltily paying for private schooling, financing her misery in the currency of his own. Her voice is soothing, well pitched and pleasantly modulated, more subtly balanced than the vocabulary she favors, and I find that I am glad I have agreed to guide her over the mountain. She speaks of her adolescence, of rebellion and flight, of how she determined she would never depend on anyone, would make her own life, unrestricted by obligations and conventions; of how she studied and came to this place to research her doctorate, all the while thinking she was free, until she realized that she was not free because she was bound to the people around her, for their suffering and oppression curtailed her liberty.

"That's why I was taking the photos," she says, rubbing the residue of the paste into her fingers and the cracked skin around the knuckles. "And those notes. Dates, names, places. Nobody knows what's going on here, the evil that's being done, nobody cares. But they must know, they must care. That is why I must get to Al Asher, so that I can get out and tell the world what is happening. This war has lasted longer than any other in the last hundred years, but nobody knows about it, nobody writes about it."

"Perhaps because it has lasted too long," I suggest softly, glad that she has seen fit to confide in me about the photos. "It is part of the furnishings of Africa, along with corruption and catastrophe and starvation and HIV and . . . " I am about to add the ritual mutilation of women, but after what we have seen I let it go.

"Well, it's unacceptable," she says, again echoing the language of Fr. Gianni.

It is an unusual word to use, 'unacceptable.' We have been accepting such things for tens of thousands of years and will probably continue to accept them so long as there are people to do any accepting. They are not 'unacceptable.' They are perfectly acceptable. Disagreeable, of course. We do not like hearing about our species' ingenious brutality while we are eating our beef and potatoes or drinking our hot gin. But we can accept it.

"People must be made to care," she adds.

Watching her in the dark of the night, I see that her face is not conventionally beautiful, either by the standards of my people or those I have read about in books, but there is something alive and warm about it. It is not a face to make a man yearn for a bed, but a face beside which any man would be grateful to wake in the morning, every morning for the rest of his life, because it speaks of hope and promise and honesty, things better seen than said and heard.

"People do care, Miss Kate." She looks at me sharply, but does not protest against my insistence on the title. "People always care. Not enough, perhaps. Less than they could, maybe less than they should. People are like that everywhere. They are careless, but that does not mean they do not care."

I feel a kind of pity for her at this point. I have little schooling and have never traveled beyond the borders of my country, but I have made many long voyages in books; and I find this expensively educated stranger, who has come from so far away and seen so much that was alien to her, touchingly naive.

"OK," she says, "so they do not care enough. But they will care more if they know what is happening. If I can show these pictures. That will teach these people a lesson."

"You cannot save the world by teaching it lessons, Miss Kate."

It is very curious to me that such an attractive young woman should remind me of Fr. Gianni, who was neither attractive, young, nor a woman, but they both deal in imperatives, both trust in absolutes, cataloguing everything in distinct files labeled Good and Evil, Right and Wrong. Perhaps it is the way of all moral codes, perhaps Fr. Gianni, Kate and the Warriors of God are different only in degree and procedure, not in kind. I speak of moral codes, because her next question surprises me. She asks, "What do you believe in?"

I am surprised, because this is the question we always ask white people: what do they believe in, above all, do they believe in God. For most of my people, not believing in God is as hard to imagine as not believing in breathing. Given the opportunity to talk to white people, they will pursue them on this matter, pointing to the stars and the trees and the animals of the earth, demanding how anyone cannot believe. I have always been careful to keep my own lack of faith to myself. In the past, it would have caused too much hurt and nowadays my godlessness would be the death of me. Reading books, reading the world, I make my own gods—something else the Warriors of God cannot abide.

"I do not believe in anything, Miss Kate," I say at length, "except that some beliefs are necessary and that these necessary beliefs are different for everyone."

"Necessary beliefs?"

"Beliefs we know are not true, but which are necessary if we are to live. Your necessary belief, for instance, Miss Kate, is that people are important."

"They are!"

"Respectfully, Miss Kate, but no they are not. I have read very many books. Look in any history book, read any newspaper, listen to any news broadcast, and you will see that people are not important. You can kill them in their thousands, their tens of thousands, let them die in their millions, and it does not make any difference. But I understand that if we are to go on with living, we must pretend people are important. It is a necessary belief."

"You haven't answered my question. You are telling me what I believe. What are your necessary beliefs?"

The way she looks at me suggests she is as interested in who and what I am as I am in who and what she is, but I do not answer her question. I suspect she would not like my response, she who is so attached to the deceiving truths embodied by mere facts. Besides, before I have time to phrase even an evasive reply, we hear the horseman and see the shape of something human scurrying toward us in the bed of the *wadi*.

❀ ❀ ❀

The child stops abruptly when she sees us, stays crouching, ready to run again, watching us, waiting to see whether we are dangerous. She is perhaps ten years old, spindle-legged, solemn-faced, her hair gingery from malnutrition, her thin body dressed in a dirty shift and car-tire sandals. Kate rises to move toward her, but stops when the child skitters back in panic. The horseman is nearer. We can hear the soft padding of hooves, the occasional crack of a brittle branch. The child huddles low, dark and spidery in the dim moonlight. I put my hand to my lips, cautioning silence. I hope she will understand that, far from being predators, we are fugitives like her. Her breath comes in light, rasping gasps, but she makes no deliberate noise, and does not move, cleaving to the darkness like one who would disappear if visibility were a matter of will.

The horseman has stopped. Has he heard us? Perhaps he is waiting for another noise, another word or wheeze or scuffle to give our hiding place away. There is no sound save the child's ragged breathing. Kate is still stooped, has not moved since she started toward the child. The cold seems more intense now that we must stay still, and I shiver slightly. Then there is a soft tearing sound, like the uprooting of a plant. It continues, vegetative, repetitive, familiar. Kate squats on her heels, looks questioningly at me. I crawl to the far side of the watercourse, the side from which the horseman approached.

I hesitate, hunkering below the wall of the *wadi*. The low moon casts blue shadows across the *qoz*. If I raise my head, I might be seen. But the sound continues, a regular, almost domestic tearing, and it is gnawing at me, eating away at the compulsion to stay still, demanding I take a decision, make a move. Then I realize what it is. Eating, gnawing, vegetative. I look over the edge of the *wadi*. The horse is a dozen strides from where I am hiding. It is grazing at a coarse clump of dry grass. There is no sign of the rider.

I look left, right, fearing he is creeping up on me, but still I cannot see him. The horse sees me, though. It shies away, whinnying before trotting off a few paces. We are lost now. Or rather found, and being found, lost. I drop back into the *wadi*, indicate that Kate and the child follow, quickly, and start running toward the mountain, bent double to profit from the precious shelter. The man will be after us. I am expecting to hear a shot, either at us or into the air to alert his companions. They cannot be far away. Men with guns and horses never ride alone. They may pretend they are invincible, but at heart they know they are vulnerable. Power is a trick, like community is a trick, like love and charity are tricks, like reading and telling stories and walking them out across the land are tricks, ways of denying death and pretending we can somehow escape. Everyone needs these tricks and it doesn't much matter what your trick is, so long as it teaches a little human warmth and pity. Pity is essential. Without pity, everything becomes too inflexible, be it a person, a government or a system of belief, and being too inflexible it will break. But for pity, you need imagination, and that is not something the men with guns and horses can stomach, because then they would imagine their own deaths as well as those of others. That is why they stay together, to avoid the moment everyone experiences sooner or later, that small quiet despair when you are alone and you know that your trick is not enough, that it will not save you, however hard you work at it.

Fifty yards along the *wadi*, I stop. Kate is beside me, the child, thankfully, a few paces behind us. There is no sound of pursuit. I raise my head again. The horse is further away, but clearly visible. It has forgotten its fright and is calmly cropping at the sparse vegetation. There is nothing else, apart from the moon, the odd tree, and motionless shadows. The horse's reins hang loosely from its neck, snagging at its leg when it moves, causing it to step awkwardly around the dangling obstacle. I laugh, stand straight, amused by my very human talent for inventing terrors of the night. Mr. Poe would have been proud of me. There is no rider, no Warrior of God, no man with a gun, only the horse. Even when they are stalking a solitary woman outside the camps, the Warriors of God and their ilk never ride alone. Even hunting a child, they would stay in groups of two or three. The horse must have bolted during the storm. Perhaps it is the horse of the Warrior of God I unseated, or has strayed from another encampment altogether. No matter. It is a loose horse and a horse is not only an instrument of attack—it is a means of running away, too.

I scramble over the side of the *wadi* and hurry towards the horse, but it bucks and trots away. I try again, walking more slowly, but the horse will have none of it, and every time I approach, it ends up a little further away. Then I feel Kate's hand on my arm. She tells me to step aside. I do as she says and she starts walking, not toward the horse, but off to the left. She does not look at it, just walks away, gradually bearing right so that she slowly describes a series of circles. The animal watches her, wary at first, wariness fading to indifference, indifference turning to interest as the circles draw nearer. When, at length, Kate is within a few feet of the creature, she squats on her haunches, and scratches lightly at the soil. The horse approaches her of its own accord. She does not move. The horse leans down and nudges her with its muzzle, not hard, but with enough force to unbalance her. She steps back, then stands, yet makes no attempt to grab the bridle. She holds up her hand. The horse stretches out its neck and nuzzles the palm. Only then does she gently scoop up the reins, stroking the animal's nose and flank, and talking softly to it. When she turns and walks back to us, the horse follows docilely.

"Where did you learn that, Miss Kate?"

"Daddy's guilt money," she says. "One of the few useful lessons I did learn at that place."

It is most remarkable. In the brief time since we first met, I have understood that Kate is not a woman for approaching things sideways. She goes at them head on, confronts rather than circumvents, but in this instance she knows not to scare the animal. The horse even follows her down the crumbling wall of the *wadi* and does not object when she tethers it to a large stone unearthed by the run-off.

We turn to the child. She is barely less shy than the horse, but does not bolt. Looking for some way of affirming our friendly intentions, I am slightly taken aback to discover that I am carrying my shoulder bag containing *Moby Dick* and the lighter foodstuff, that some blind instinct made me grab what was most vital before we fled from the phantom horseman. I offer her food, leaning forward, careful to keep my distance while I trickle a handful of groundnuts and *sim-sim* into her outstretched palm. She eats hungrily, pushing the mixed nuts and seeds into her mouth, licking her hand clean afterwards. I ask her name. She does not reply, so I repeat the question in all the languages of this region, but still nothing is forthcoming, only a gesture toward the bag. I slide the bag toward her and she digs out more groundnuts. For the first time, she smiles, a cracked, uncertain sort of smile, ingratiating but not obsequious. When she has finished eating, Kate and I move a little closer to her. Only then does it occur to me that she cannot speak. Fearing the worst, I show her my open mouth and waggle my tongue, smiling afterwards to indicate that there is nothing menacing in my strange behavior. She finds this comical, laughs, and shows me her mouth in return. I am relieved. Her soft pink tongue is complete, nothing has been extracted. There is no sign of damage about the throat, either, no bruising or rope burns. Whatever prevents her speaking is not

physical. It is in her head. Whatever she has seen, whatever or whoever she is fleeing from, it has been enough
to stop up speech.

"What are we going to do?" asks Kate, surprising me
with her implicit faith in my judgment. I am, after all, merely
the man with a headful of books, novels to boot, yet she
appears to have accepted that I merit some respect, am in
some sense a leader.

"Fetch our things," I suggest, "then sleep."

"I mean about her."

"What can we do? If she wishes to come with us, she
will, and we will do our best by her. Nobody else is going
to look after her. And perhaps she will look after us."

Kate looks doubtful, but I am not being wholly friv-
olous in this. If the child stays with us, we will be like
a family: man, woman and child. She will be the cement
holding us together and we will need that strength if we
are to survive what awaits us.

When I return with the bucket and other bags, Kate
and the child are sat side by side, hunched against the
sandy wall of the *wadi*. Kate has her notebook braced
against her knees and is sketching with the nub of a pencil
while the child leans forward, peering over Kate's forearm
at the emerging picture. I glance at the drawing, briefly
distracted by the firm movements of Kate's hand before I
realize that she is sketching a cartoon of me trying to catch
the horse. It is crudely done, but as the figure creeps forward, crouching like Fagin in one of the old illustrations,
manifestly about to pounce, the expression on the horse's
face is so perfectly absurd that I have to smile. The horse
is looking out at us, its eyes protruding with alarm, its
lips puckered in a small ellipse of disbelief as if it is whis-
tling, calling upon us to witness the indomitable folly of
a predator so patent that only a creature of unparalleled
imbecility would let him catch it. I would wager that the

drawing is the truest thing in that notebook. The child seems to agree. She glances at me and giggles slyly.

"You make a parody of me, Miss Kate. I thought you only had time for what is true."

She looks slightly put out, though whether she is vexed by the title or because I have caught her in a moment of inconsequence, I do not know.

"I'm not obsessed, you know," she says. "I have my lighter side, too."

I do not reply, but however light she fancies her lighter side may be, I think she is obsessed. I know because I am obsessed, too.

The cold is even more acute now. There are no saddle-bags on the horse, but there is a rough wooden saddle, and below it a red blanket. I scrape a hole in the sand of the *wadi* and all three of us curl up under the blanket. The child refuses to go in the middle, still requires the security of being out on the fringes, so it is Kate who lies between us in the warmest spot. During the night, I wake to find that Kate has rolled against me and is gripping my arm. It is not a sensual gesture, just an instinctive reaching out for human comfort in the cold of the night, but the fragility and neediness of one otherwise so strong and certain is touching. Later, I disengage my arm, taking care not to disturb her sleep.

❖ ❖ ❖

We wake to a warm, velvet wind, the tail end of a distant storm twisting out of the desert to the northwest, as soft and supple and impudent as the breath of angels. It curls around our bodies, caressing us back to life, brushing away the alarms of the night, like the kindly hand of a fond lover. If there is any divinity beyond our own mad dreamings, it dwells in moments like this gentle wakening in a wild land when even the most turbulent of elements can collude in an illusion of tranquility. Too often the simple gifts of being alive are lost in the clever, inventive mess we make of living, yet they are the only creed we need. God is an accident of nature, not an architect. But men are always looking for some distant father, a draftsman who will take responsibility for the disorder of their own lives.

We breakfast on a handful of groundnuts and a cup of water. Whatever robbed her of speech, the child has not lost her trust, and sleep has lent her a dream of safety. From the way she sits beside us, eats with us, then stands when we saddle the horse, it is clear that she has adopted us, has decided to confide herself to our care, the situation assumed with all that quick-witted pragmatism we shed so rashly with the advent of adulthood. What, though, is her name? Take a child from the wilderness and you cannot simply call her The Child. Again, I try to make her speak, telling her our names, writing them in the sand with a stick, but she only smiles and turns aside when I offer her the stick. I tell her we will call her Mara. It means woman in the language of the north and is the name of the mountain. She seems pleased with her new identity, smiling with such sweetness that I despair of a world that can conspire to steal a child's voice.

"You do not believe people are important?" asks Kate, watching me with a look that is almost mischievous.

"I do not believe anything except that we must reach the mountain today. We have been too lucky already. We cannot carry on like this. And the nuts and seeds will not last another day."

Something in the tone of my voice, or the words themselves for all I know, catches Mara's attention for she looks at me anxiously, as if perhaps she has been too hasty in entrusting herself to people who can do so little to help her, people who are in as much need of help as she is. I make a mock sad face and am gratified by her laughter. Kate laughs, too. Already, we are functioning like a small family, papa fooling around for his womenfolk. I know this play.

The horse is too weak to carry us all, being little more than a bag of bones held together, very provisionally it would seem, by a thin hide of chafed skin patched with sores where the saddle has rubbed and the horseman's heels have goaded it. Kate rides it first to test its temperament, then takes Mara in front of her, setting off along the *wadi* while I follow with the sagging waterskin and our stock of food. It is much like my old life, only now I carry a more immediate form of nourishment and my companions have not been conjured from fiction. They are, as Kate would say, 'real.'

The mountain rises above us, purpled with frayed sheets of debris and veined with dark green runnels of vegetation. To the west a broad trail climbs toward the last village, zigzagging between abandoned fields from which the stones have been tossed onto the track to make a haphazard paving. This is the obvious ascent, but it is the way the Warriors of God would take if they ventured up the mountain, so we stick to the *wadi*, hoping the gully that feeds into it will offer a way up. I fashion a sling from a strip of my shirt and carry a couple of stones in my waistcoat pocket, intending to fell a dove like I used to with Jemal when we walked north, but we see no living thing. I have read that before times there were many large animals here, even antelope and bustard, but they have all been shot by Saudi tourists who call killing sport, taken from this place in much the same way that they poach our teachers and doctors, so that the land is emptied of both its natural and cultivated fauna.

Toward noon, we reach the first foothills and stop to let the horse drink from a pool of muddy water. Only after a few minutes do we notice the smoke. Behind us, to the southeast, a long concentrated spiral coils into the sky, black against blue like the twisted trunk of an unnaturally tall tree. Mara becomes agitated and will not be comforted by Kate or myself. She gestures at the smoke and makes small, inarticulate noises of distress. In truth, we, too, are discomfited. It is far away, which means we should be safe for the present, that the men with guns and horses, one group of them at any rate, are not near us, but we know what that smoke means—and so does Mara. No doubting now what robbed her of her voice.

"You see why I must go to Al Asher?" says Kate, gazing at the smoke, the ghost of another village. "Such senseless violence."

She is wrong again. I am beginning to think she generally is. Violence is never senseless. There is always the sense of the victim's feelings and the sense of human inadequacy on the part of the perpetrator. But I do not contradict her because I suspect Kate does not really believe this violence is senseless. She believes it can be stopped, which means it has a discernible logic in which we may intervene, some sense beyond the mere insanity of man. Besides, there is something about her stubborn wrongness that appeals to me. She is like one of those endearing characters in books whose fortunes the reader cares about in large measure because they keep on making a complete hash of everything they do.

"You did not know, Miss Kate," I say, by way of apology for not having warned her when we first met. "But when the phones do not work that means somewhere is going to be attacked. We have learned to fear this thing, for we do not know where they will attack next, only that it is about to happen. I should have told you before we left. It will continue for several days now."

"You could know," she says, "or guess."

She sounds almost angry and I sense that the mood of the morning and the nascent complicity we enjoyed last night are both spoiled. This little family is still a fragile thing, not an elective affinity but something forced upon us by circumstances. The chemistry is all wrong.

"Know what?" I say.

"Where it is going to happen."

"But it is random, Miss Kate. You might as well guess at God or gamble on a camel facing Mecca at prayer time."

Mara sidles closer, slips her hand in mine, her eyes still fixed on the plume of smoke, which crumples and unravels as it rises higher in the sky. I am about to suggest we move, if only for her peace of mind, when Kate says something that stills me.

"It's not random," she says. "There's a pattern to it. You can even map it. They're drawing straight lines in the sand and the lines all lead east, to the capital and the sea. They are corridors and the people are being cleared from these corridors. Once you know the route, you can tell pretty accurately where they will go next."

It fits. Men like the Warriors of God do love a straight line, something unwarped by human eccentricity. But I do not see what these lines have to do with disputes that have their roots in ancient rivalries and recent dearth, disputes that, above all, have become an argument of the edges against the center, and I tell her so.

"Have you read your government's Encouragement Act?"

I have not. There are limits, even to my reading. If reading is alimentary, government acts are the toxic plants of the printed word.

"My government is not in the business of encouragement."

"Oh, but it is. There's oil here. Uranium, too. Zinc, silver, copper, tungsten, gold, no end of mineral wealth. Diamonds, emeralds, other precious stones. This is a rich country. No, don't laugh. I mean it. It is all 'a sacred gift to the faithful,' as your government has it. But to get the riches out, they must get the big companies in. And the big companies want to be 'encouraged': tax and customs exemptions, guaranteed land tenure, and no risk of disputes with local people. They've learned that lesson in Nigeria. Take a map, locate the mining concessions, then draw straight lines between those places and the capital, and you will be able to predict the pattern of these attacks. To get what's in the ground out of the ground, they need to get people off the ground. And then, to get it out of the country, they need a secure transport corridor."

I do not know what to say to this sudden speech, only that it is better to say nothing. Kate has grown heated, is speaking to me, at me, as if I am personally responsible. This is often the way with people who believe in a cause. Righteousness feeds off itself and the passion to put the world to rights provokes its own gratifying anger, an anger that, once aroused, is not particular about its target. It is Mara who saves me from Kate's conviction, just as she previously saved me from her need to ferret out the convictions of others. The child is gently pulling at my hand, glancing anxiously at the tattered tail of smoke fragmenting in the deep blue sky. It is enough. I pick up our bags and indicate that Kate should lead the horse. Glancing back, I take one last look at the smoke and the line Kate claims it is tracing across the land, a ghost road shaped by the shadow of a creature we cannot otherwise see, and I begin walking again.

⊠ ⊠ ⊠

We proceed more slowly in the mountain, but the sense of progress is greater than on the plain. When the world is flat, one can walk for hours without apparently getting anywhere; but because everything is concentrated in a mountain, the distance already climbed comes as a constant surprise. It is the same with stories. An aid worker once gave me a book that he said was "just an airport novel." I did not understand what he meant until I read the book and saw that it was flat, like an airport. It showed many things, but the characters rushed through events like people on a plane that races down the runway and never takes off. I like books that tell me things, climbing steeply and cramming a lot in. In the end, they cover more ground.

There are no continuous paths in the gully, only stretches of trodden ways where jackals pass or a shepherd has been in the habit of moving his flock between scraps of pasture. Piecing these patches of path together, we weave our own trail, teasing out a narrative of landscape from the fragments left by previous passers-by. The first night, there is no shelter, nowhere we might light a fire that would not be visible from the plain. I want to save the remaining groundnuts for the uplands, so we grind wild finger-millet and thorny grass seed into a thick gruel that swells the belly and tricks it into believing it is full. Likewise, I tell Mara stories that will seem to seal and heal the pain of what she has seen, hoodwinking the heart with words of another world that make the forgetting easier. It is the trick that took me safely out of my own disrupted childhood. I do not know whether she understands what I am telling her, but the sounds seem to soothe her, and she falls asleep on the blanket before we have prepared the ground for a bed.

Kate and I sit for a while watching the sleeping child. We do not speak and perhaps it is better thus. In the silence, we are repairing the damage done by those heated words of this morning. Moving on, making camp with Mara, Kate and I work together with a common purpose, but when we speak we seem compelled to declare our differences. There is an anger inside Kate, an anger she keeps in the space where I store only sadness and maybe a little despair, and when each is aired our respective resentment and resignation seem inclined to consume one another. We will not survive this journey if we let antagonism take over. Yet there are some things, some fundamental instincts that we share.

The next morning, Kate sets Mara on the horse alone, claiming it will not last long carrying two people in this terrain, but I suspect that, like me, she prefers to walk. Mountains are best approached on your own two feet. Only then can we appreciate just how far we have climbed and use the mountain as a means of locating ourselves in the world. Time before, when I still visited the upland villages, I would frequently leave the main track and follow byways, or ways where there was no path at all, so that I was in sort telling myself a new story about the shape of the mountain, one that was different from the story told by other men. I often got lost, sometimes hazarding my very life. Indeed, on one occasion, I would almost certainly have wound up as vulture meat had a shepherd not happened to find me. But despite the danger, I was happy because I was finding my own crooked way through the world, making it up as I went along, and measuring myself against a scale that has more meaning than the usual yardsticks of money, power, and possession. If Kate opts to walk, it is for her own good, not for the well-being of the horse. This is what I choose to believe.

In the early afternoon, the rain returns. This is a harsh, violent land, and the weather is harsh and violent, too. Our rain never patters and splashes and puddles and mizzles. It is a brutal beast that seethes and spits and builds so relentlessly that you feel it will keep growing until it tears the world apart. Fr. Gianni always beat us after a storm, for it put him in a terrible temper, the world growing so dark, the rain drumming so hard on the high tin roof of the classroom that no learning was possible, and his crisp lessons in virtue and vice had to be cut short. On the mountain, we cower together in the lee of an overhanging rock, but within minutes we are wet through and the gully is ankle deep with rushing water. We climb higher, away from the turbulent central channel, scrambling over the loose, slick rocks and unstable stony soil, Kate dragging the unwilling horse while I steady Mara, half carrying her up the slope. There is nowhere to go, though, nowhere to hide. In the end, all we can do is cringe into the mountain and wait for the fury to exhaust itself.

Later, when the storm has passed and we are climbing again, we hear a distant sound that stills us and makes the horse skittish. We cannot see it, but there is no mistaking the muffled *whomp-a-whomp-a-whomp* of the blades. There are only three helicopters in this place. One is assigned to the peacekeepers, but is rarely used because when they go to the depot they are told there is no fuel or the pumps are broken. Only once have I seen it fly, when a white man came to visit, an important man with an important job to do, which he did in an afternoon, then went away, and we never heard of him again. The second helicopter is the property of a prospecting company, but that has been grounded since the war got big again. The third belongs to the government. It is called a gunship and is sometimes used when one of the larger villages is attacked. We wait, exposed on the bare flank of the mountain, wait and watch and listen, but nothing appears and eventually the sound fades away, and we walk again.

Tomorrow, we will pass the last village. Beyond that lies an unmediated landscape, bereft of even the broken goat tracks that crisscross this gully. This evening, we are fortunate. Toward the head of the gully, we find a small cave, the walls blackened with soot. It is even furnished with the hard dry trunk of a long dead tree left behind by the herdsmen who have now been driven away. Dead grass spotted with desiccated goat pellets is scattered about the floor of the cave. Heaping it together under the tip of the trunk and tearing out the still-dry center pages of *Moby Dick* for extra kindling, I make a small fire against which we can warm our extremities and dry our clothes. I cook *kisra* on a flat stone and tell Mara more false stories of hope and escape, stories that I know are not true, but which are necessary. I still do not know if she understands the words, but I believe something is communicated by their sound because she is calm and soon sleeps, so deeply that she does not wake when a spark from the fire spits against the cracked, calloused sole of her foot. Kate and I sit and watch the small flame of the fire as it licks around the stump of the tree's root.

We are sitting next to one another when I happen to glance over my shoulder, my attention drawn by a rustling that I hope might be a rodent or some other edible creature. Behind us, our shadows dance together, projected onto the rough screen of the cave wall by the flickering light of the fire. Animated by the wavering flame, they dart across the dark rock, occasionally flaring over the roof of the cave, weaving and prancing in unison, though staying slightly apart throughout. There is no rodent, no life that might supplement our provisions, but the shadow dance makes me uneasy for some reason, so when I stand to push the dwindling stump into the embers, I take advantage of the movement to sit on the far side of the fire, opposite Kate. She does not seem to notice, is lost in thought, her wraith-like shape dancing alone now, a jittering spirit jailed in a magic lantern. At length, she stirs herself and speaks.

"The helicopter," she says. "Do you think they were looking for us?"

"We are not important," I say. "They would not waste fuel on us."

"I did make one call," she says. "The day before we met. I called a friend at home, told her what I was doing, and why. Maybe they know what information I have."

I watch her, once again feeling a kind of pity for her naïveté. In the orange glow of the fire, her skin looks artificial, like the flesh of a drawing in a color textbook. She really believes that what she has to tell is important, that a few pictures and a few facts can change the world. It is a conviction that can only hurt her.

"Even if they know," I tell her gently, "they do not care."

"They must," she says, imperative again. "They must understand that if people know what is happening here, really know, know the evil that's being done . . ."

It is too much for her, she is silenced by the burden of her own belief.

"You think a testimony to horror is useful, Miss Kate? People know that evil is being done everywhere, all the time. And they live with it. They may not like it. But they live with it, they get on with their lives."

"I can't forget what we saw back at the village," she says. "And what I've seen before. I won't forget it. I won't allow myself to forget it."

"It is not forgetting. But other things go on and they are more important. Laughter, love, hope, they do not disappear because people are suffering, even because many people are suffering. They carry on just the same and we all prefer to look at these things because the hurting is too big for us to control. Even if the whole world sees your pictures, nothing will change. The government knows this. They are not looking for us."

As it happens, I am wrong. The government is looking for us. The Warriors of God are looking for us. The helicopter is looking for us. Above all, the pictures, or pictures very like them, will change something. But it is not what Kate hopes will be changed. They will be read another way, another message taken, a lesson 'learned' other than the one she wants to teach.

"That's what I hate about Africa," she says, with sudden intensity. "The fatalism. You are all just so accepting, so bloody tolerant . . . What's the matter? You don't like what I'm saying? It's true, you know."

She is more sensitive to dismissive gestures than to dismissive words. I only raised my chin slightly, perhaps clicked my tongue, but it was enough to stop her.

"Tolerant is not a good word, Miss Kate. And even if it was a good word, it is not a word to describe what is happening here."

"What do you mean it's not a good word? How can you say that? It is the basis of everything."

I do not point out that she is now promoting what she was previously criticizing. Consistency is a witless virtue valued by dullards and I understand her attachment to tolerance in general, even if she complains about it in the particular. In books, tolerant is always a good word. I accepted this unquestioningly for many years until the war got big again and outgrew its old clothes so that it needed to dress itself in religion. Then I thought about all the occasions when we talk of tolerance and decided it was a nonsense. That this man bends the knee and that man bows the head; that this one is brown, that one pink, this one pale, that one dark; that this man must trim his foreskin and that man must grow his beard; that this man has a partiality for introducing his generative organ into one orifice and that man a fondness for delving into another . . . there is nothing to tolerate in these things. If you take pleasure from spitting in my *chai* or have a regrettable tendency to lift your leg and break wind while I eat, yet I like you well enough not to make an objection, there is some tolerance in it. But the rest is just a way of making us feel good about ourselves. Tolerance is not a virtue. It is only the absence of intolerance, and that should be a given, something understood, not striven after or enjoined on others. If we cannot avoid the futility of intolerance, there is really no point carrying on at all.

"A good word used badly then. Most of the time, there is nothing for people who call themselves tolerant to tolerate . . ."

"There is here," she interrupts. "You've seen as much as me. But I'm willing to bet, if it ever stops, your people won't punish the guilty ones. It's always like that in Africa. It's always reconciliation and the guilty ones go free. That's what I mean about being too tolerant. Tolerating injustice."

I do not reply immediately, I know all this speaking gets between us, that we are better together when we are quiet together, but there is a fierce need in Kate's gaze, which I take to be a desire to understand that is quite as ardent as her compulsion to condemn. The gaze is almost a glare now, but I speak nonetheless, choosing my words carefully.

"You know, Miss Kate, before all this began, I mean before the raids and feuding got worse, we lived a different sort of life here. It was not perfect. Very far from. But there were good things about it. Among my people, when a child did wrong, he was not scolded. Instead, he was told a story to help him understand how his bad actions had affected others. The consequences for the community were more important than the consequences for the individual troublemaker. . . ."

"Well, it's not good enough!" she snaps, interrupting me before I can elaborate.

At first, I am shocked. The ferocity of it! But then I cannot help myself. It really is beyond my control. I start to laugh. Not at her, not directly at her, but an image has come to mind of Kate berating all the people she has met here, giving them a good telling off because they are not quite up to the mark. White people are so improbably out of place wherever they go that I wonder whether they are at home even when they are physically at home.

In their books they are nearly always misfits or are mis-fitted by their enemies until the author contrives for them an implausibly happy ending and a pleasing comeup-pance is engineered for the villain. Permanently displaced people, they are obsessed by guilt and punishment, as if by ascribing blame they can place themselves in the world. I sometimes suspect culpability is one of the main resources they require of our ramshackle continent. Aside from the minerals and raw materials, we give them a grati-fying sense of guilt, and they mine it with all the eagerness of a greedy man digging for diamonds. Where the yearning for punishment comes from I do not know. Does it go with the guilt like a dust jacket goes with a book, a means of both protecting and proclaiming what lies inside? Is it merely what is left over after you have done away with God, a lingering desire for a punctuation point defining the end of a sentence? Or maybe they require legal redress because they are frightened of spontaneously confronting wrongdoing. That is not the case here. Africans may be easy-going, but we are not, as Kate claims, 'tolerant,' and the child's indulgence is not always blandly extended to adults. Go to a crowded market in my country and shout "Thief!" and everybody will be jumping all over each other in an attempt to literally stamp out the problem. But there is no sense of punishment, nor time to cultivate an aware-ness of guilt. Problem identified, problem solved, all done and dusted. There is little justice in it, no question of extenuating circumstances, and scant consideration as to whether we have got hold of the right culprit, but at least we do not waste our days endlessly brooding about iniq-uity. If we did, we would never get anything done at all, for there is matter enough to hand.

"Why are you laughing? It's not funny, you know."

"Perhaps that is when we must take care to laugh the most," I suggest.

Strangely, she is not angry, but appears to have relaxed, which makes me think she did not really need an explanation of why I was laughing. I even begin to suspect she likes being challenged, enjoys the fact that somebody disagrees with her vehemently moral views and finds her just a little bit ridiculous. I hope it is so. There is a sneaking tenderness stealing into my admiration for Kate, and I would not want to feel this way about someone who could not enjoy being a little bit ridiculous.

"Necessary laughter?" she says, smiling at me, as if our relationship is one of long standing, a friendship in which the foibles of each are familiar, and have become a part of the intimacy, prized as much as the positive traits. "Like necessary beliefs?"

She is right. Laughter like certain soothing beliefs is necessary. Both are essential when there is no justifiable reason for them to be there. I could almost commiserate with the Warriors of God were it not for the fact that they need to write their faith on the bodies of others. They may believe they have a hold on immortality, but I very much doubt they ever laugh. Certainly, Jemal was never one for laughing. Despite our former closeness, I have to admit that he was a solemn, slightly dim child who has grown up to be a solemn, slightly dim man. The only time I ever saw him laugh was when Fr. Gianni fell through the tin roof of the toilet block trying to catch two boys abusing themselves, and that would have made a cat laugh. None of us knew what the Sin of Onan was, but we all reckoned that if it got Fr. Gianni falling through the roof of the toilet block on a regular basis, it was a very good thing indeed.

Right now, I am equally positive about Kate's insight and what I take to be her descent from the moral high ground. It moves me, like her defiance and compassion did before. Better still, she does not press me for a response to her question or earlier accusations. Mara stirs in her sleep and it is like a suggestion, for we speak no more, but lie beside the small fire, slightly apart but together in the dark of the night.

I stay awake for a while, wondering what it is that I find so appealing about this difficult, prickly, wrongheaded woman who demands so much of herself and those around her, and even more of the world at large. She is attractive enough, but no more beautiful than many other women better suited to my station in life. Nor is it because she is in some way exotic. Exotic is another bad word. It is not what is alien, but a fantasy of what is alien, like erotic is a fantasy of sex. Neither of them has anything to do with the real thing. Kate is the real thing, a real woman exerting a real fascination. In the shimmering light of the fire, her face is in repose, relaxed despite the burden of indignation she carries around inside her. Yet it is no different from her waking face. When they sleep, the faces of most people disclose a defenselessness long since lost in the waking world, but in Kate's face there is no difference between the waking and the sleeping selves. She does not dissemble or place a protective mask between herself and the world. She is simply herself. I think perhaps it is this concentrated honesty that attracts me above all. That and the fact that she does not admit the possibility of those foolish distinctions we normally draw between people. Though we do not rightly understand each other, she has accepted me with all simplicity. Ordinarily, when I have spoken with white people, I have nearly always felt that they are secretly pleased with themselves for talking to me, as if they have overcome a barrier, or proved something to themselves. That is not the case with Kate. From the very beginning, she has not permitted that there can be any barrier. We are just two people who have chanced upon one another in unusual circumstances, circumstances that pare away everything else, leaving only big questions and the tricky little matter of survival.

❊   ❊   ❊

The village has not been burned and there is no sign of violence, but it is empty and the departure must have been hasty because many things have been abandoned, among them items that may yet save our lives. There are blankets and pots and pans, a tinder box that will be a better firelighter than stones, a blunt ax head with a broken shaft, and even a cache of food: a bag of water-melon seeds, a cracked cake of *sim-sim*, a handful of dusty dates, a pound of broken rice, and a pot of groundnut meal. I pack what I can in a blanket while Mara and Kate wash in a deep pool at the foot of a small waterfall where the young boys used to swim.

Wherever she comes from, Mara has been lucky in one thing. Her people cannot have been marked by either the new religious fervor or the old reserve, because she bathes naked, unconscious of her sex. Kate wears only her underclothing and swims from one side of the pool to the other, ducking her head, then kneading her scalp with her fingertips before clambering onto a rock beside the falls. Water drips from the bagged seat of her underwear as she hoists herself onto the flat rock, pivoting forward on the heels of her hands. The muscles of her back are small but more clearly defined than is normal and the deep crease of her spine is flanked by unusually long shoulder blades that foreshadow the inward curve above the globes of her buttocks. It is a very beautiful back, too beautiful to be regarded dispassionately, and I turn aside, pretending to busy myself with the search for other items the villagers have left behind that might be useful to us. But what I find is no comfort at all.

I see something dark on the edge of the village, to the north, where the trails taper into the untenanted mountain. I see what it is, know what it is, but I have to go and look more closely because it should not be there, and I would that it were not. There is no gainsaying it, though. It is a small pile of horse excrement. Looking more closely, I realize the ground around the huts is dappled with the imprints of horses' hooves. Not a large party, maybe three, four, a half-dozen mounted men. But the tracks should not be here. Our own horse has not strayed, there were no horses or mules in the village before, and the donkeys were unshod. Moreover, the droppings are fresh and have not been broken up by the preceding day's rain.

I do not tell Kate what I have seen. Problems are not halved by sharing. They are made bigger, growing into the available space. If everyone kept their problems to themselves and dealt with them as best they could, the world would be a quieter place. No healthier, perhaps, but quieter. Besides, if my fears prove true, she will learn soon enough. Men with horses have been here recently, but they have not come to burn or loot. Perhaps they were sheltering from the storm. But that does not explain why they are so far up the mountain. Nor why they have continued to the north, where there are no villages, only jackals and baboons, and the great crater where there is said to be a lake that smells of sulfur. What could bring them up here apart from us? Are Kate's pictures as important as she claims? Or is it me they want, the man they could not kill?

Kate asks if I am going to wash. It was not my intention, not after what I have seen, but I do not want to alarm her, so I strip down to my undershorts and hurriedly rinse myself in the muddy shallows at the edge of the pool. With luck, the men will not be returning this way directly, though I hope they will come this way later, for I do not want them roaming the uplands while we are there. I have promised more fires, more *kisra*, and beans and okra, too.

Washing while Kate lies in the sun on the rock on the far side of the pool, I am reminded of Jemal and his hygienic heaven with the virgins lathering up his lap. I cannot help but smile at the memory, even though that original mirth may yet be the death of me. He was so earnest in his description, he could see it all, every last soap sud, was convinced God would get him out of this dreadful place and into another place where all his frustrated adolescent longings would be satisfied if only he believed hard enough. A necessary belief then. In the end, I do not really know why I mocked him. I was suffering, too, and— as fantasies go—his dream was beguiling enough. But then I already had another place where all my longings were satisfied, a private place into which I could retreat and remake the world in different shapes. I did not need God, and soon enough, Mihad and the rudely interrupted discoveries we made together in the book hut would confirm my suspicion that, if there was to be any business with lovely ladies, it would be happening in the here and now, not the hereafter.

Coupled with the tantalizing image of Kate's back, the thought of lovely ladies washing private parts excites me, and I am obliged to turn away to conceal my perturbation. I sink into the shallows, hoping the cool water will dampen the impudent autonomy of my impenitent member. As with many things, women are better equipped in these matters, for their desire does not declare itself with such reckless indiscretion. The loose clothing of desert dwellers is no help at all, either. Often enough, I have been obliged to sit down suddenly when a lovely lady has walked by. Do not let anyone tell you the allure of a woman is impaired by wearing a *tobe*. It leaves too much to the imagination and consequently keeps a man of sensibility in a state of enduring agitation. To distract myself, I think about the dung on the perimeter of the village and all it means for us, but the sense of danger only intensifies my arousal, and

I really do not know where to put myself. Once the light changes, though, I find an effective remedy in nature.

At first, one might not notice it save for the sudden drop in temperature. Then the light fades and the world goes gray, as if a cloud has formed, except the grayness seems to magnify the things around us, giving the impression that we are seeing the world through clear deep water. I turn toward Kate, all thoughts of paradise and private parts forgotten. She has sat up, is hurriedly pulling on her dress. Mara is cowering beside the water's edge, oppressed by the sudden darkness, like a small stricken animal, only this animal is gifted or cursed with consciousness, and is darting anxious glances at the world around her, aware that something menacing is happening. I look up into a violet sky and see that the sun is almost covered by a big black disk, like a loose lid on a hot cauldron.

"No, don't look!" shouts Kate, leaping forward to take Mara in her arms and shield the child's eyes. "It's the eclipse."

"What eclipse?" I ask, lowering my eyes in response to her urgency.

"Of the sun," she says. "People were talking about it before I came. I'd forgotten the date. But I knew it was due. The moon is passing across the face of the sun. It's a near total eclipse. But if you look at it without protection, it can blind you."

I have heard nothing of this, though I have read something like it in a book, something I did not properly understand. With the incorrigible curiosity of the confirmed reader, I would like to look again, but the authority in Kate's voice is enough to prevent me. She tells me to follow and leads Mara to a *neem* tree that stands a little way above the pool.

Mara is trembling despite the calming touch of Kate's hand. The trembling diminishes though when she sees the shadows of the leaves. They are watery shadows, transparent but still distinctly shadows, and they are overlaid, one on the other, so that each seems to be a shadow of the shadow beyond it, though none can be clearly separated from the preceding specter. There are thousands of them, many more it seems than there are leaves on the tree, and interspersed with the shadows of the leaves are countless tiny images of the sun, again overlapping like pale golden clouds piled on top of one another. The pattern is captivating. Even Mara, who was so dreadfully alarmed and cannot understand what is happening, is entranced by the beauty of this closely concentrated spectacle. For my part, I see in the countless tiny suns a counterpart to reading. Books, after all, serve the same purpose as this *neem* tree. They are the shadow makers of the mind and, in the shadows they cast, we can see the shape of the sun, see something which is otherwise unbearable to watch.

The feeling that something magical has happened persists long after the eclipse has passed and carries us through the remains of the day as we climb away from the village, washed in the weak light of a sallow sky. Even my fear that men on horseback are somewhere ahead of us cannot lessen the sense of wonder. Even the sound of the helicopter. It is more distant this time, muffled by the folds of the mountain, but can only be a few minutes flying time away. No matter. This day is suffused with a state of grace that danger cannot dispel.

We camp on rising ground in a stand of trees. Kate does not question my refusal to light a fire, despite our thin dinner of cold groundnut meal gruel. It is as if she trusts me, even in a decision that entails discomfort. In lieu of a physical heat, we warm ourselves with memories of the shadow of the moon and gaze at the sea of pea green grass that has draped itself across the *qoz* in the wake of the retreating rain. It is patched with splashes of red where no seed has survived and stretches away like a patterned carpet to the tall wide wall of the pale blue horizon. In the east, above the horizon, the high sky darkens to a dense deep blue. To the west, the sun sets, gilding the great desert with a gold that cannot be mined nor spoiled by the petty trafficking of mankind. The night is cold.

▨ ▨ ▨

Beyond the trees the groove of a shallow valley has been scooped into the shoulder of the mountain. At its head, a wall of dark rock spotted with pockets of trees and scored with runnels of paler rock rises to a serrated ridge that must be the rim of the crater. There is a way into this crater, which was once used for pasture, and on the far side at least two ways out leading to the northern flank of the mountain and the slopes above the crossroads. I have never been this high before and do not know the way, but I can see several deep creases in the wall that might mark the southern passage. First, though, we must traverse the valley, which is bare and dry, and filled with a dust so fine that it covers our feet at every step, in places rising to the horse's hocks, causing it to stumble in the hidden holes that pock the underlying rock. Mara is amused by the staggering progress of the horse and giggles every time it trips, but Kate is uneasy, fearing the child might be injured, so she stops and makes Mara dismount, saying it would be wiser to walk until we reach the head of the valley.

That is when the bullet hits.

It is unnaturally quiet in this powdery place. There are no birds, no rodents, no jackals or baboons, nothing but small bright blue butterflies that seem unbearably fragile in the heat and dust. Despite the silence, though, we do not hear the shot. Perhaps it is the shock or perhaps nature is rebelling against such an aberrant sound,

swallowing up the report in protest at the noisy impertinence of men and their madness in a place so far removed
from their habitual playgrounds.

We do not hear the shot, but we see its results, see all
too well the sudden blossom of blood, the horse reeling to
the left to escape the angry red flower that has sprouted
a fraction below its withers. Maybe Mara hears, though.
Even before the horse falls, knocking Kate aside, the
child is scrambling through the dust to the west, swim-
ming against the dirt of the world toward a wild dream of
safety. The horse kicks at the air, twists and lashes out,
trying to right itself, but raises only a fine white cloud
under which it disappears, a large, indeterminate brute
thrashing blindly at its own eclipse.

I do not remember throwing myself down, but I am
lying on the ground, and my back is sodden where the
waterskin has split. The blanket carrying what we salvaged
from the village has burst open at my side. The skin of my
hands and forearms is white with the talc-like dust. There
is a shout, the crack of another rifle shot, heard this time
but not seen, then the men on horses appear. There are
three of them, riding off the eastern ridge, one with his
rifle in his hands, another with some sort of short spear
or lance, a type of weapon I have never seen here before,
the third holding nothing but the reins of his horse, riding
hard and ahead of the others, leaning forward, spurring
the animal on.

Kate is the first to react. She is on her feet, running,
not away from the horsemen, not west like Mara, but at
them, making directly for the man in the lead. At first, I
think she has lost her reason, is blinded by fear or dust
in her eyes, but if there is any dust in Kate's eyes, it is
emotional not material. When the leading rider sees she
is heading for him and veers to the right intending to pass
her, she also changes direction to cut him off. It is like with
her photos. She thinks she can stop the madness of the

world and she thinks she can stop three armed horseman, just by placing herself in front of them in a display of sheer bloody-minded determination. All I can think of is what was done to the woman in the village. If they catch Kate alive and I cannot reach them, or reaching cannot resist, it will be the lips that they will go for, and all her words of protest at the world's injustice will never be articulated again.

I snatch the broken ax from the blanket and begin running after her. I am faster than her, but she is already fifty paces ahead. I will not overtake her before she reaches the first horseman, but still I run because in such circumstances that is all one can do, run away or run forward. Standing still is not an option.

The horsemen have splintered from their common course, are spreading out so that they cover the middle part of the valley. The leader is still bent low, galloping hard and fast, too hard and fast. He should know better, but then this is unfamiliar ground for him, too. Doubtless he sees dust like hard-packed sand, a safe surface for speed. The horse catches a foreleg in a hidden hole and plunges forward, pitching the rider head first into the dust. The horse pedals air, the man lies still, Kate turns aside and rushes at the second rider, the man with the gun.

He reins in his horse, raises the rifle, fretfully jiggling the bolt as if fearing it might jam. Kate keeps running, heedless of the gun. I catch up with her as the man takes aim. I hit her hard with my shoulder, sending her sprawling in the dust. The shot splashes chalky powder in the air several feet behind us. The man gropes at a small leather purse hanging about his neck. His horse is bucking, the purse flapping wildly. Kate is rolling over, trying to get up, spitting dust and blood from a split lip. The man fumbles a bullet from the purse. There is the same awkward pantomime with the bolt before it slides into the breech. The horse shies right, forcing the man to grab the reins and steady it. The gun is raised again. But already the ax is twisting through the air, spinning neatly with a balance that has more to do with the weight of the head and the length of the broken shaft than any particular skill in the way I hurled it. It hits him in the chest, blunt end on, hard enough to make him cry out and knock him from the saddle.

The third Warrior of God is behind us somewhere, but there is no time to tell where, no time to look for the spear, for the felled rider is already on his knees, scrabbling for his gun in the dust. I am not aware of running across the ground, nor of grappling with the man. The next thing I know, he is underneath me, and I have my hands around his throat, and all my weight is bearing down on him, my shoulders and arms pushing his head back. The pressure is so great that his face disappears in the dust like a pebble in water, but I keep hold of him, keep pressing with my thumbs, pressing harder and harder, my entire strength concentrated in those two digits. For a while, he scratches at my face, then his hands form claws trying to tear apart my arms, but he is losing his strength. I seem to blank out for a few moments or rather lose awareness of what is happening, but I am still astride the man, his head is still held fast, deep in the dust, and my thumbs are pressing down so hard that it feels like they will snap. The man's left leg is flapping weakly, like the broken wing of a dying bird. His hands have already given up the unequal struggle. Then he is still.

The sound of angry shouting brings me back to myself, makes me realize that I have heard nothing the entire time I've been astride the man, nothing but a wild white roaring in my ears. Kate's voice cuts through the white noise, as sharp as a jackal's bark in the dark of the night. There are hard expletives, gasping, the tearing of cloth, more swearing and tearing and grunting. Somehow she has reached the third horseman without being run through by the spear. The horse is rearing, the man is holding on with one hand, and in the other he has Kate's dress, torn from her back in the struggle. According to Kate, the man is a copulating natural son with an unnatural fondness for his mother, a hemorrhaging onanist, an unclean pudendum, and many other things besides, a course of enlightenment he does not have the leisure to contemplate, because she keeps throwing herself at the side of the horse, trying to claw him from the saddle. Her bra has been torn off, too. The triangle of her bare back is streaked with sweat and dust. She is screaming and clawing. And it is hard to tell who is more wild-eyed with terror, the man or his horse. This must be his worst nightmare come true, a demented naked woman whose only desire in life is to tear his eyes out, and there is no guarantee the tearing will stop there, either.

He lashes out with his right leg, catching her in the chest, sending her spinning sideways back into the dust. But he knows better than to push his luck any further. He may be a Warrior of God, he may be a man with a gun buckled to his saddle and a dagger strapped to his arm, he may even have a spear somewhere if it's not broken, but he has come to grips with a very she-devil, and he knows, without a shadow of a doubt, that the only rational thing for a real man to do in such circumstances is to show a clean pair of heels. He drops the dress, wheels his horse about, and gallops away to the south, back to the trees, the village, the track and the plain, back to comrades in arms and the comfort of numbers, and far, far away from wild women without shame or skirts.

Kate is sitting up by the time I reach her, still using such shocking language that I wish I had met her before I went to the orphanage. Words like these would have had Fr. Gianni on the first plane home, all his sanctimony packed in a small satchel at his side, his lips pursed in a pout of disapproval so tight that you could insert a bicycle pump in the other end and inflate him like a balloon until he floated away, a bubble of censure ready to burst at the prick of a pin. I sink down beside her, take her hands in mine, and start laughing, madly it seems, because it stops Kate's stream of expletives, and she squeezes my hands, then reaches out to touch my cheeks. Only then do I realize that I am not laughing, not really, but weeping, weeping because of the terror of it all, weeping because I have just killed a man, weeping because I would that Kate were right and all this might be ended with a little publicity, weeping for the horror of what I thought was about to happen to her. I lift my hands to touch her face as she is touching mine, to stroke and hold and soothe, the proper function of hands, some tenderness to banish the horrible tactile memory of a throat being crushed by book-muscled fingers. Who knows how far the touching might have gone had Kate not spoken. But one word from her stems my tears and stills my fingers—Mara.

We hasten across the valley of dust to the west, the direction we last saw her taking. It is easy to follow her traces in the valley, it is as if a large beetle has crawled through a plate of flour, but once we cross the western ridge, the dust stops abruptly, and a slope of bare broken rock drops steeply into a scree-filled gully. There is no sign of her, so we start picking our way down the slope, slowly because there is no stable footing here, and several times one or the other of us falls or slides a few feet along landslips of grit. Then I see a small quaking figure crouched behind a boulder. Her arms and legs are striated with cuts from where she has fallen and she is crying, gulping back her sobs between gasps of breathless panic. Kate reaches her first, but Mara scuttles away, as if even these arms are no longer to be trusted. I try to approach from the other side, but being cornered only makes her terror worse. We sit and wait, hoping our presence will be less threatening if prolonged and peaceable. Waiting is not wise. There is no knowing how far the third horseman has to go to fetch other men like himself. Maybe the Warriors of God are already riding into the valley of dust, maybe any minute now they will appear on the ridge above us. But there is nothing else to do, only wait. Africans are good at waiting. To my surprise, so is Kate, she who is so impatient to put the world to rights. Equally surprising is my own indifference to her state of undress. She is all but naked, yet concern for Mara temporarily suppresses what, only the day before, had seemed so irrepressible.

After a little while, I start telling stories, false stories of hope and escape, necessary stories, and whether Mara knows the words or not, they seem to work again, because before nightfall Kate is able to approach her and cradle her in her arms, then coax her back up the slope into the valley. Both horsemen are dead, the first having broken his neck through his own reckless haste, the second strangled by my bookish hands. Our horse is dead, the horse of the man I killed has disappeared, but the one that tripped is still alive, lying on its side, occasionally paddling hopelessly at the dust, making soft plosive sounds of distress. Its leg is broken.

I give Kate my shirt, keeping the waistcoat for myself, and hand her the bag of food, telling her to go ahead, to wait for me at the head of the valley. She ignores the bag, says she wants to bury the dead men.

"We don't have . . ." but her look silences me. The lovely green of her irises has clotted and deepened, pinching the pupils into bitter black pricks that I find a little frightening. Below her hard, dark eyes there is a tension about the set of her mouth that suggests a capacity for spitting pure venom. This is not a woman I recognize. Even back at the truck, when I first taxed her with taking photos of dead people, her defiance did not amount to the kind of malice I can see in her now.

"So I can stamp on their graves," she says.

"There is no time," I murmur, avoiding her eye. "The wild animals will see to them. Take the bag, take Mara, go."

She still glares at me with those small eyes of hate, but when I reach out and take her hands in mine again, she does not reject the gesture. A pulse of emotion passes between us, a flicker of something soft and warm and human. The rage is still there, still coursing through her like a current of electricity, but it is earthed, tempered by contact with a feeling that is more diffuse and less fierce. Perhaps the thought of wild animals feeding on the bodies comforts her, too. Eventually she accepts the bag, retrieves her notebook and memory card from the torn dress, and leads Mara away. When they are out of earshot, I unsheathe the dead man's knife and cut the horse's throat. I should take some meat, too, but there is no time for butchery. I collect the other man's knife, the salvage from the village, and the spear which I find buried in the dust near the rag of Kate's dress. But I do not take the guns. I want no guns, even now, even here, and have no real notion of how to use them even if I did. I can find no water and do not dare wait any longer.

It is dark by the time I join Kate and Mara. The moon is rising and it would be as well to continue walking, but in this landscape even the moon is not enough. We need daylight, like whoever may be pursuing us needs daylight, so we sit and wait it out, not sleeping, only dozing, and that very fitfully. Nobody eats, even though I try to persuade Kate and Mara to have some dates, and we are too dejected to talk about what has happened. Instead, we just sit and wait and watch and feel the thirst build through the cold of the night.

Toward dawn I notice that Kate is shivering, sat upright, hugging herself in a fruitless attempt to stay warm. I hesitate only briefly, then sit behind her, putting my legs on either side of her waist and wrapping her shoulders in my arms, so that my wrists cross below her throat, like a hand mime evoking the fluttering wings of a bird. I have not forgotten the arousing beauty of her naked back, nor the gratifying warmth of her bosoms pressing upon my upper arm. I can feel the slight rise of her buttocks against my groin and the imprint of her hips on the underside of my thighs. She is so close that I can smell the must of her and see the blush of a fading birthmark partially hidden by the hairline on the back of her neck. But the embrace is a sexless gesture nevertheless, and I believe it satisfies a sexless need in both of us. Mara slips between Kate's legs, as if it is the most natural thing in the world, and rests her head on Kate's breast. Kate holds the child and I can feel them both relaxing into me, and for all the fear and hunger and thirst, I am strangely satisfied.

❖ ❖ ❖

It was danger that brought us together, danger that has driven us up the mountain, and it is danger that eventually jostles us unceremoniously into one another's arms. Otherwise, it would not happen. Even if we had met in another place at another time, a place and time in which the tender marrying of white skin with black was not condemned, we are too far apart in hope and in despair to be a likely couple. But when two people are pursued across a mountain by the Warriors of God, some coming together is inevitable.

The crater is broad, maybe two or three miles across, not flat and rocky as I had imagined, but filled with undulating grassland intermittently punctuated by the isolated crowns of small umbrella-like trees. There is no dust, but we proceed cautiously because the slopes are pitted with holes, some as deep as the height of a man, many concealed by the long grass. The way into the crater was easier than I had feared, easier than I would like. Transhumance in times past has made it almost path-like, but what bothers me most is that the gap is wide enough for two horsemen to ride abreast.

Mara has a talent for survival. I do not mean she is likely to survive. She is weaker now, we often have to stop to let her rest, and twice I have had to carry her on my shoulders, albeit briefly because I am also tired. But she has a talent for survival in her head. It may have robbed her of speech, yet she got away from a place I would wager few others escaped, and today she is as affectionate and easy with us as ever she was, as if the terror that drove her stumbling down that steep slope and then kept us at bay when we found her was a fleeting, forgettable mood. A child's trust is an astonishingly resilient thing. Thirst may yet put an end to it, though. Thirst may put an end to everything.

We can see no sign of the lake and are making our way toward the far side of the crater, the only place where the rising ground is high enough to conceal a large body of water. I cannot say whether we will get there, though. It is not far, but the fear and exhaustion of the preceding days, and the physical exertion of the fight in the valley of dust have weakened us badly. Even if we make it to the high ground, there is no guarantee that we will find water. In that case, we will not have the strength to get out of here. As I remember it, the elders, who used to come to the crater with the cattle when they were children, spoke of two exits, a clear cutting like the way in, and a steep dangerous gully climbing to the northern crest. I do not recall where the easy route lies, but I have it in mind that the gully is near the lake. We might make it through the easy way even without water, but for all I know, we are walking away from safe paths, could as well be sealing our fate with every weary step we take.

It is midday and we are at the center of the crater when the sound reaches us.

Whomp-a-whomp-a-whomp . . .

It is much nearer this time and getting closer.

By chance, we are beside one of the holes. It is shallow and narrow, too small for all of us, but I urge Mara into it, placing the tell-tale red blanket with our belongings at the bottom of the hole. She needs no second bidding. If nothing else, this child understands the value of hiding. I tell Kate to hurry, to find another hole, somewhere, anywhere to conceal herself. The rhythm of the blades is increasingly distinct, but the helicopter still cannot be seen. I rip handfuls of long grass from around the hole and scatter them over Mara. Still the noise grows, still I cannot see its source, or even decide precisely what direction it is coming from. It seems to be all around us, which is not possible, there cannot be so many helicopters approaching from all sides. Even Kate would not fancy her testimony that important. Though the helicopter is not inside it yet, the crater must be catching the thud of the blades, and sending the sound back and forth, so that the echo swirls around us in disorienting circles.

I hide the spear, bucket and bag in the undergrowth, and search for somewhere to conceal myself. Kate has disappeared. I do not know which direction she went. *Whomp-a-whomp-a-whomp!* I begin to panic, start running blindly. There are no holes nearby, no trees, not even a rock. *Whomp-a-whomp-a-whomp!* It is a terrible thing to be hunted from the air, the helpless sense of being the prey of something larger than yourself compounded by exposure. I trip in the grass, fall flat, scramble to my feet, plunge on. *Whomp-a-whomp-a-whomp!* Kate's face appears above the grass a stone's throw off to my left, shouting for me to go that way. *Whomp-a-whomp-a-whomp!* She drops out of sight. *Whomp-a-whomp-a-whomp!*

The helicopter rises over the rim of the crater, still distant, but so close to the rock that it seems to be skimming the surface. An illusion, no doubt, but not a happy one. It is the government gunship. I want no government gunships skimming surfaces. Better that those bounders went into orbit. That is the strongest word I have for them, bounders. I never did learn the habits of swearing. It is rare in the books I read and I am not inclined by nature to spoken profanities despite the many profanities of my lifestyle. Vulgarity in words is often merely vulgar, but vulgarity in life is life itself.

Whomp-a-whomp-a-whomp!

That's what I thought, at least, until I heard Kate's ripe vocabulary. Right now, I am beginning to regret the vulgar life that has brought me to this pass and have a compelling urge to take up vulgarity in words. Cursing as best I can, I bend double, running toward the place where I think Kate disappeared.

Whomp-a-whomp-a-whomp!

"Blasted bounders! Blasted bloody bounders! Blackguards!"

Whomp-a-whomp-a-whomp!

"Damn and blame you, you dirty bilge drinkers. Galoots, flats, toady men, dogs, swabs!"

Whomp-a-whomp-a-whomp!

No knowing whether they have seen me, but I run hard, still stooping, still swearing for all I am worth, which is not a lot in the present circumstances.

Whomp-a-whomp-a-whomp!

"A plague on you, you dastardly carpetbaggers! Dishclouts! Scurvy knaves! Camel jockeys! Scabs! Dunghills! Lummoxes!"

Whomp-a-whomp-a-whomp!

"Avast, you lily-livered, lubberly coxcombs!"

Whomp-a-whomp-a-whomp!

"Sapheads! Pox-mongers! Rascally scoundrels! Blast your eyes, you bounders!"

Then the ground tips away below me so abruptly that I am pitched headlong into a hole. Kate shrieks with shock as I land on her and, for a moment, we are a tangle of limbs. The sound of the helicopter is clear now and more easily localized. It sweeps back and forth, combing the surface of the crater. Are they looking for us? Or worse, for a landing place? Perhaps any moment now they will find flat, stable ground, and troops will be pouring from the belly of the beast. The hole is deep and concave on one side. I press myself into the overhang, so that I will be invisible from above, then pull Kate after me, pushing her against the wall of dirt.

We are pressed tight against one another and, as I peer from under the overhang, trying to get a glimpse of the helicopter, I can feel Kate shaking at my side. Can Kate be shaking with fear, this oh-so-bold woman who tackles armed horsemen, collects photos of the dead, is ready to take on an entire government, confront an entire world of evil? Is this possible?

I turn to look at her. She is not shaking with fear. She is giggling. Her whole body trembling, her bare breasts showing above the loose neck of the overlarge shirt. Then the explosion comes. Two snorts, desperate attempts to contain it, but to no avail. She is howling with laughter. It is real laughter, too. It is not hysteria or terror, but genuine, delighted hilarity.

"Your face," she manages to splutter, "when you fell. Your face . . ."

"My face?" It is strange, but even in such circumstances a pratfall is funny. Perhaps especially in such circumstances. Perhaps Kate has come round to my way of thinking concerning a world full of irredeemable evil interspersed with a few fleeting moments of humor and happiness and love.

"Rascally scoundrels!" she screams.

But that is as far as she can go with it. Words will not do. Only laughter. She is helpless. If she was not dehydrated, I believe she might wet herself. Laughing like crazy, kicking her heels, drumming her fists, convulsed with great gales of mirth. Me, too. I do not notice it beginning, but before long, I am shaking with laughter as well.

"Bounders," she squeaks, helplessly, as if the word were the wittiest in the world.

The helicopter continues to trace long lazy arcs across the crater, but it cannot stop our laughter. In fact, when it swings close, only fifty yards or so behind us judging by the sound, our glee achieves a new pitch. We are laughing so hard that we might even knock it out of the sky. Wouldn't that be wonderful if all we had to do when confronting men with guns and helicopters and bombs and all the other elaborate paraphernalia we have developed for dismantling one another was simply to get together and laugh them out of the skies? Has it ever been tried? Would any army in the world be proof against ten thousand ordinary people laughing at them?

When and why our laughing stops is as unclear as when and why it began, for I cannot believe it was only a bit of cursing and the sight of my face that set it off, but stop it does, because suddenly we are in one another's arms. Kate smells of sweat and grime and dirt and dust, a smell more fragrant than any distilled in a sterile laboratory stocked with essences and diplomas. Her lips are dry and cracked and salty with blood, but the kiss is sweet and tender, so clumsy and kind that it is like a testament to the marvelous ham-fisted loving of ordinary people doing their best in an imperfect world. It would not get you very far in a book. We might well be on top of a volcano, but the earth does not move for us, and the eruption of passion is no fiery spectacle lighting up the heavens. It is not that sort of kiss. Too mucky, too maladroit, too much like two people at the bottom of a hole with a helicopter gunship hovering overhead, but all things considered we are not doing too badly. We hold onto one another with such desperate passion that it seems no Warrior of God, no helicopter of soldiers, no world of madness can tear us apart. This is the way to do it, laugh them out of the skies and then kiss to fill the silence.

Kate and I are out of here.

We have gone to earth.

OK, let's go, please.

❋   ❋   ❋

Fr. Gianni told us all about it. Secret, satanic messages. They are everywhere, concealed in publicity posters, imprinted on the packaging of consumer goods, woven into the lyrics of popular songs, relayed in magazines, movies, logos. . . . The risk of coming into contact with such contaminated material ought to have been pretty slim at the orphanage, where publicity posters, packaging, popular songs, magazines, movies, and logos would have been thin on the ground had Fr. Gianni not seen fit to remedy this puzzling oversight on the part of the people behind his diabolic conspiracy. He had files full of them, countless examples collected by like-minded men who could see the devil everywhere they looked, never wondering whether the devil wasn't in their regard rather than in the things they looked at. Like I say, he was a very funny man. Only much later, long after I had left the orphanage and filled myself with books, did I make the connection with stories. Every story gives out hidden messages, too, except the author does not know what they are. Storytellers may think they know what they are saying, may say what they want to say well, but the involuntary revelations they are also making must always be a mystery to them. Only readers detect the accidental messages and interpret them, bringing them to life, only readers know in the end what is really being communicated.

Sometimes, this alchemy of reading seeps into what imbeciles call the 'real' world. Yes, I know, Kate, who only has time for what is true, is a type to talk about the 'real world,' Kate for whom I am learning an unlikely love, but love does not mean we cannot admit imbecility in the loved one. We are all imbeciles, all sadly cracked about the head, each perfecting our own peculiar form of imbecility. Love accepts other forms of imbecility than one's own, that is all. When the alchemy of reading seeps into the so-called real world, we decode messages other people are giving out, messages they do not know they are giving out and would not understand were they told. I do not know what messages Kate reads in me, the secrets that have made that frantic kiss a seal of something deeper, but I believe I understand something of what I read in her.

Kate is a pusher. Reaching a door, all people are either pushers or pullers. Some instinctively push, some automatically pull. Say one is a pusher confronted with a door that opens in rather than out, most people will simply say, "Ah, this door must be pulled, not pushed," and act accordingly. Not Kate. She keeps pushing, pushing and pushing and pushing, determined the door will open the way she wants it to open. It sounds stupid, mad even, but it is marvelous to watch, and I suspect that the people who make a mark on the world are those who *will* have their way, who *will* push no matter how many doors need pulling, regardless of the consequences. I am sure she would deny it if I told her, but Kate is a pusher in every respect of her person. She has certainly pushed me over a threshold I would not have crossed on my own.

The helicopter does not land, but continues to scour the crater until whoever is inside it is satisfied with the wind they have made, and the noisy bug pulls away, arcing over the crater's rim, and dropping out of sight down the mountainside. This is the way of men. We make a lot of wind, then when we have done with our blustering, we take off, leaving patches of flattened grass and a few frightened witnesses. Or, in the case of Mara, a witness who seems to think this is some great game staged for her benefit. When we resurrect her, she is smiling happily, and brushes away the remaining grass, like somebody found and glad to be found after a game of hide-and-seek. Whatever happened to her village, the helicopter played no part in it.

We walk for another hour, stopping frequently as the ground climbs more steeply, but when we breast the final rise, our fatigue and my own growing anxiety that there will be nothing there all fall away. The lake is the deep blue-green of a bee-eater's feathers, so bright and still that it is like a lid, like the circle of the moon was a lid, only this time what it covers is cold and, rather than defying the human eye, compels immersion. We rush down the brief slope, stripping off our clothes, and plunge into the icy waters. Mara does not seem to notice that Kate and I are naked. We barely notice it ourselves. It is only right. There can be no modesty between us after that kiss, a kiss of such intimacy that I can still taste her on my mouth as I dive under the surface. The water is so cold that it takes the breath away and, as I rise from the depths gasping, I realize that it does indeed have a faintly sulfurous flavor, a fact that would have had Fr. Gianni swooning with rapturous indignation. Whether it is the work of the devil or not, I could not say. All I know is that it is delicious and that, once we have dried ourselves in the sun, our skins seem sealed with a fresh integument.

After clearing the grass from a square of earth beside the water's edge and enclosing it with a low wall of stones, I make a fire. Kate rinses white dust from the okra and Mara entertains herself by tossing stones into the lake, where they float for a few seconds before sinking. There is a sense of peace here, a sense of something achieved, though that easiness is false. We are still hunted. Moreover, there is the memory of the man I killed. In situations like this, you do what you have to in order to survive. No more. No less. I have killed a man. I had to do it, but the fact still stands beside me, like an unwelcome guest reminding his unwilling host that something is owed to him by the rules of hospitality. I do not feel guilt, but when you have killed a man you are changed, you know it is possible. Perhaps that is what the Warriors of God are doing, experimenting with the possible.

As evening approaches, I watch the purpling shadows spread across the crater, searching among the emergent relief for some sign of the safe way out. It is not here, though. There is nowhere that might conceal a clean cutting onto the far side. There is, however, a gully, steeper than any we have climbed so far, lined with loose rock and the very occasional clump of scrub. If we cannot find the easy way out, that treacherous looking scramble may be our only option. Worse, in the morning it will be in the eye of the sun. We have water now, but we cannot carry it up such rough ground in an open bucket.

Once Mara is asleep, her breathing deep and regular, Kate and I steal away from the fire and stroll up toward the edge of the lake's basin, the move mutual and unvoiced, even by any signal of the eyes, and we make love in the long grass. Our lovemaking is as clumsy as our kissing was when we were hiding in the hole, but the very awkwardness of it makes it all the more human. I am not some puffed-up stud from one of those flat airport novels, polishing his distended rod prior to a record-breaking bout of press-ups, and Kate is not a romantic heroine ticking off synonyms for illumination, cataclysm and ignition. Nothing flares, floods or explodes. We are just two people holding onto one another on top of a mountain for fear of falling off.

The only bombast to accompany our lovemaking comes courtesy of a couple of jackals howling at one another, their cries echoing across the crater, so that it seems we are surrounded by a pack of the creatures, either approving or deploring this commonplace confederacy of bodies. I do not know which, nor do I care.

Kate gets a fit of the giggles again when I look at her reprovingly and say, "Miss Kate," as if it is she who is howling, giving voice to the operatic ecstasies expected of an airport novel heroine, sensation clad in so many superlatives that it has all the impact of a damp sponge. She is too wise for that, though. She knows. Sex is not about superlatives, there is nothing consummate about consummation. It is simply a means of making a common map on which frontiers are fluid and overlapping rather than fixed and definitive.

Perhaps all women understand this, just as they appreciate better than men the simple fact that the world is not made of discrete bodies, but of bodies connected to one another, and that the real beauty and value of living is to be found in the links between things. It is when we break these bonds, with others, with ourselves, with history and with a proper appreciation of consequences, when we fail to cohere that we become capable of doing all the mad, bad, stupid things we do.

The words 'Miss Kate' are no longer a provocation, but a jest telling us how far we have come together.

❧ ❧ ❧

Kate has a tidy mind. Perhaps that is where all morality comes from, tidy minds sifting the accidents of living into boxes arranged by color, size and contumely. But tidy minds save time, too. Her insistence that we pack our few possessions before retiring means that, come morning, when we have to leave, we need only wrap the loose items in the blanket, shoulder the bag, and go. And we do *have to* leave. Very urgently. Their white shirts and robes are clearly visible to the southeast. A score of horsemen filing into the crater. No time for finding safe ways out now. We have got to escape as best we can. At least they should not see us as easily as we see them. My shirt and waistcoat are made of cheap pasty-colored cotton, the type used for convicts' uniforms. No Warrior of God would accept such material. Warriors of God wear costly white cotton bleached of all impurities. We can see them clearly, but with luck, Kate and I will be little more than pale smudges against the beige rock, while Mara's smock is so multifariously dirty that it might have been designed as camouflage.

We make our way around the lake to the foot of the gully. It is even steeper than I had thought and I wonder briefly whether this is the right gully. There may be no way out at the top, just a drop plunging off the other side. It is possible we will not even be able to reach the top and are simply setting a snare for ourselves. Perhaps we should hide, but there are no holes this side of the lake, the scrub is too sparse to screen us, and the grit too hard to dig ourselves in. Besides, if the horsemen find the ashes of our fire, they will not leave till they have found us, too.

Mara skips ahead, still happy. She has not seen the horsemen yet and while she is moving there is no need to scare her. Kate keeps glancing up at the wall of the crater, as if that is where the danger lies, but I take no notice, and hurry her along the middle of the gully. There is no path, but it seems sensible to stay in the central channel until some obstruction forces us onto either flank. The loose stones are tiny here and at first the walking is easy, but the gradient soon gets so steep that with every step we slide back half a pace. Before long, we are sweating and breathless, and Mara is no longer skipping. Our haste seems to have infected her with anxiety. She keeps looking up, left and right, as if expecting someone to appear. Kate is gasping, more than might be explained by the exertion.

I ignore it. We have to keep moving. We are going too slow. We must move faster.

An obtruding rock blocks the central channel, forcing us up the western flank to skirt the obstacle. Afterwards, we do not return to the central line. There is another rock fifty feet ahead, one twice my height, and another beyond that. We start zigzagging up the slope. The stones are bigger, almost small boulders, but less tightly packed, and several times we dislodge individual rocks, sending them somersaulting into the gully. We have barely begun climbing, but already we are scrambling, sometimes crawling, grasping at tiny sprigs of dead weed, anything that will offer some small purchase, though most are so frail that the slightest tug uproots them.

I glance back into the crater. We are above the rise defining the far side of the lake. I can see the bright white shirts of the Warriors of God bobbing across the grassland. If they knew where to look, they would see us, but for the moment they are concentrating on the ground immediately around them. If the man who escaped from the valley of dust is with them, he will know the dangers of riding too fast up here, so they will be looking out for pitfalls, and are perhaps also expecting to find us hiding in the long grass.

We are a hundred, a hundred and fifty feet above the bed of the gully. The drop is almost vertical. Scrambling up, often as not on all fours, the gradient is dissembled, but once revealed, it is startling. It startles Kate. She stops, presses her face to the ground, no great distance as she is already on her hands and knees. I take her elbow, drag her up. We keep moving, climbing until our ascent is blocked by a long sheet of rock stretching away on our right to the top of a small cliff halfway up the central crease of the gully. The sheet of rock is about fifteen feet high, almost perpendicular, its smooth wall inset with smaller stones of a harder consistency. We start edging along the rock, using the stones as footsteps and handholds. They are insecurely set and sometimes come away in the hand, but the moving is easier, especially for Mara who is lighter and nimbler than Kate and me, and is soon several yards ahead of us. Then Kate, who is behind me, stops. Not resting but rigid, her feet set on two stones, her head and hands pressed to a brief and very slight incline in the main rock. Her eyes are shut, her face streaked with grime and sweat.

"I can't," she says.

"Can't? Can't what? Quickly, please, Miss Kate, we must move."

But even the name does not stir her.

"I can't. I'm scared."

I am flabbergasted. Kate? Scared? This is not possible. Yet she looks very like a woman who is genuinely scared. Her complexion has turned pale below the patina of dirt, her lips are quivering, her legs trembling.

"I am scared, too. That is why we must keep moving, before they see us."

"Not of them. I don't mind them. The height. I'm scared of heights."

Is this what drives her to want to save the world, fear of the vertiginous depths and heights of human folly? There is no leisure for being scared of heights, though, moral or material.

"Nothing will happen," I tell her. "We just have to keep moving, one step at a time. We will soon reach the end."

"You don't understand! I can't. The height."

I know I do not understand. Other people's fears are always inexplicable unless we share them, and even then there are many variations on a common theme. The Warriors of God fear the unappeasable power of womankind, the villagers fear the violence of the Warriors of God, I fear their faith, any faith, religious or secular that puts belief above people; all these fears come from the same source, a dread of extinction, yet they are mutually impenetrable, differing in both degree and manner.

"You are frightened of falling?"

"I am frightened of everything! Of falling, of being here, going forward, going back. Just the height!"

It is not only sweat streaking the dirt on her face. Tears are squeezing between the lids of her eyes and her upper lip is striped with snot. There is an acrid, ammoniac smell as well, though whether this is consequent on her sweat or some more humiliating discharge, I cannot tell.

Mara has turned to see what the problem is—and she has seen it: not Kate and her fear of heights, but the men in the crater. They are not far from the lake, have split up to cover the ground approaching the rise. They will see us soon. With a wave of my hand, I indicate that Mara should continue. She looks at me, I nod encouragement, she moves. Kate, meanwhile, is pressing herself so hard against the rock that I half expect her to knock the mountain down. There is no doubting that she is a pusher. I think if God got in her way, she would push Him over, too. A story comes to mind, one I heard many years ago at a roadside *chai* stall, told by a foreign teacher trying to explain his lack of faith. It is not strictly relevant, but it is the best I can do. I tell it to Kate.

"There is a climber, Miss Kate. He is very, very high in the mountains and very, very far away from every help when he trips on a steep slope and topples head over heels down toward a precipice very, very fast. Just as he tips over the edge, he manages to grasp the exposed roots of a shrub clinging to the edge of the cliff. He is hanging there, dangling over the drop, with enough energy to hold on, but not enough strength to pull himself back up. His grip is getting weaker, the soil holding the shrub to the cliff is crumbling, and soon he knows he must fall."

Kate whimpers, the acrid smell gets stronger, but I press on.

"After a while, he says: *Is anybody there?*

"There is long silence, then a voice comes from the heavens, a deep rumbling voice that echoes around the mountain like thunder. *Yes, My son,* says the voice, *I am here, the Lord God Almighty. Trust in Me, My son, have faith, and I will save you. That is all you need, a little faith and you will be saved by the Lord God Almighty. Have faith, My son, have faith. Let yourself go, let go of the shrub, do not fear the abyss, only let yourself fall, and My heavenly angels will swoop down and catch you.*

"There is an even longer silence and then the climber says quietly: *Is there anybody else there?*"

At first, I am concerned that I have misjudged it. I do not understand this fear. Talk of precipices and abysses and falling may not be precisely what is required. But then I see the trembling has shifted from Kate's legs to her shoulders and, though this time the muted laughter may have something of hysteria in it, she informs me, with admirable brevity, that I have at least one thing in common with the Warriors of God—my mother was innocent of any legal contract with my father.

"OK, Miss Kate, let's go, please."

She consents to move. Inching her foot forward, she finds another toehold, then slides her right hand along the smooth rock, fumbling for something to grip. I guide her hand to a secure stone, move along myself, help her next move and her next, until she murmurs that it is all right, she can do it herself, and we are again edging along the band of rock. Mara has already reached the end and is crouching beside a large boulder at the top of the cliff, anxiously watching the men below. I do not look back. I do not need to. Warriors of God are ever willing to announce their progress to the world. There are excited shouts from below, the sound of galloping, a noise I have learned to hear with dread. They have seen us.

It is marvelous the inspiration these shouts provide. No supporters in a football match ever urged their team on to greater effect. We are not exactly scampering along the rock face, but we move, even Kate, with a new fluidity, and the motion is such that when a stone comes away in our hands or falls from under our feet, our momentum carries us onto the next. Only once does one of us slip and it is me rather than Kate, a stone giving way under my back foot as I am stepping toward the next, so that for an instant I am supported only by the uncertain handholds and the painful purchase of my knees against the bare rock. I glance down then, get an inkling of what Kate might be feeling, for the drop is unequivocally vertical at this point. But the stones in my hands hold and I am able to pull myself back onto a bulge that is almost broad enough to be a ledge.

I look back to see if my near fall has revived Kate's terror, but it seems she has not even noticed, she is concentrating so hard on her own progress, eyes fixed on the rock immediately in front of her, determinedly ignoring anything more than an arm's reach away. Beyond her, I can see the green disk of the lake, as smooth as a plate of painted steel. The Warriors of God have crested the rise and are riding round the lakeshore to reach the foot of the gully. Why? I still cannot fathom the purpose behind this determined pursuit. True, Jemal has promised he will kill me, a promise made more imperative by my recent display of reticence concerning its implementation, and there is always Kate with her penchant for exposing the ways of men who would really rather remain unexposed, but to go to such lengths. These men know full well that anybody abandoned in the wilderness without help will, in all likelihood, die anyway. It is a technique they have often used when clearing the villages. They do not need to hunt us down. Time and heat and thirst and hunger will do the job well enough without their help. Yet still they

come. Perhaps they have killed so many that they are running short of prey, or perhaps their single-minded quest
for a God that will address all their doubts means they
cannot support what most of us learn to support so well,
the simple habit of failure. They have tried to kill us once,
twice, and will keep on trying till they succeed because
failure compels you to look inside yourself, and looking
inside themselves is something they would really rather
avoid. I can understand that. If I was them, I would not
want to look inside myself, either. The emptiness might
move me to vertigo, too.

By the time we reach the end of the band of rock and
rejoin Mara, the Warriors of God are at the foot of the
gully. Several spur their horses up the slope, as if they
really hope to ride after us, but there is no way a horse
can follow here. Others dismount, ready their guns and
start shooting, but their aim is very, very far from true.
The Warriors of God are not accustomed to distant targets.
They kill from close range. Only a lucky shot will harm us.
Even so, I am not persuaded it is entirely wise to dance
about exhibiting our private parts at them. That is what
Kate is doing. She has taken off her underpants, which are
sodden with sweat or urine, and is jumping up and down
waving the wet cotton at the Warriors of God, chanting
insults detailing their uncertain parentage, the preference
she has discerned in them for seeking refreshment from
a donkey's genitalia, and their remarkable resemblance
to the terminus of a camel's alimentary canal. What she
does not know is that, though my shirt is large, it was not
designed to contain the agitated dancing of a generously
proportioned young lady. Every time she leaps in the air,
her bosoms bounce free from the loose neck of the gar-
ment, and every time she lands, she gives the Warriors
of God a brief but vivid glimpse of her lower belly. In any
other circumstances, it would be a magnificent sight, but
I really think that, in this time and place, when all is said

and done, a measure of decorum might be more prudent. She is, of course, delirious, so relieved to have overcome her fear and reached the end of the band of rock that she is unaware of what she is doing. At least, I suppose she is. It must be said, though, that for such men as these, with their cutting ways and crippled emotions, there could be no better or more traumatizing taunt than the sight of a very vital young woman flaunting her vitality as immodestly as she may. I would dearly love to sit back and watch Kate do her worst, but someone among us must make a pretence at good sense, and I do not trust Mara to do the job. She is staring at Kate, her mouth wide open, her jaw slack, her countenance cast in an expression pitched midway between incomprehension and admiration. I wish Miss Austen was here to describe the scene. It is not the customary matter of her fictions, but she would dissect the emotions with a precision I can never match.

Bullets continue to ricochet off rocks and several horsemen are still trying to find a way up the gully. One forces his horse at a slope so steep that the animal rears then topples back, tipping its rider from the saddle. A man after Kate's heart, he is a pusher who has discovered that, if you keep pushing, the world will push back, and the world is a lot bigger than you. Others are more cautious, taking it easily, encouraging their steeds along the line of the gully, only climbing slowly. They must be discouraged. I move Mara away from the large boulder. She still cannot take her eyes off Kate, but does not resist or try to get up when I set her down beyond the firing line of the Warriors of God. They, meanwhile, are so busy with their guns and horses, not to mention the appalling spectacle of Kate and all her parts, that they do not see me hunker behind the boulder. Big shoulders, strong arms, blessed are the readers for they develop powers they never know they are learning. The boulder rolls back briefly, but once I get a good grip on its underside, I only have to heave it a few inches to breach the lip of the indentation where it has been resting, after which gravity does the rest. It tips over the edge of the cliff and tumbles down the gully, dislodging other debris as it goes. The Warriors of God scatter, wheeling their horses around, leaping aside, though in truth I do not know if they are more perturbed by my boulder or Kate's breasts.

"OK, Miss Kate, let's go, please." She does not hear me, though. She is still gleefully hallooing at the men below, turning to display her posterior with a pert flip of her fingers on her hips. I think perhaps they did not notice the boulder. If ever she gets away from this place, Kate will have left her mark. Not on the politics of murder, but on the minds of the men who are its agents. There are some among them who are so devout that I doubt they will ever sleep again after what they have seen. I am none too sure I will myself. "Miss Kate, I think in your country you say there is a time and a place for everything. Miss Kate? Excuse me. Miss Kate!" But it is only when I swing the shoulder bag in front of her, the bag containing her memory card and notebook, that she is brought back to herself. Kate has a mission. I half believe it is the only thing she really cares about. Certainly, she has no time for personal safety. She stays where she is as she tucks various portions of her anatomy back into place, disdaining the irregular shots that are starting to coalesce again. If ever they catch her. . . . No, I do not want to think of that.

We resume climbing. Thankfully, the gully is shallower here. The stones are larger, better anchored, and hopping from one to the other is much easier than that fraught, clinging, creeping progress along the rock face. We stop frequently to watch the men below, but they do not seem inclined to follow on foot, a fact that does not greatly surprise me. Men who dream of immortality rarely care to walk. It is all too human an activity, too earthbound, too physical, too tied up with the small, visceral narratives of living in the here and now, which is why it is a proper complement to reading, because both are ways of connecting with the world. Readers are insatiably curious about the world and all its ways, we want to know everything, want to immerse ourselves in the many terrestrial pleasures of being and doing and watching and tasting and touching and listening and exploring paths trodden by other people, so we read in order to live, trying on lives we do not have the time, talent or leisure to live otherwise. Likewise, walkers are avid for life, seeing in every path another possible way into the world. We cannot pass a turning without regretting the trail not taken, wondering where it goes, who made it and why, fearing we are missing some intriguing mystery in the landscape it traverses. Fascinated by the fleeting magic of life, readers and walkers want to go deep within the world and discover all the possible worlds within it. We are people of the day itself, not the day after, the opposite of that emperor of China who built the wall and burned the books and would not walk up the mountain, but resolved he would ride because riding was the prerogative of the gods. Could anyone declare more clearly their denial of life? First he builds a colossal barrier, then he closes all the gateways into other worlds! He was another dreamer dogged by the desire for immortality, grasping after permanence in a world made precious by transience, too long-sighted to see what was immediately in front of him or to apprehend what makes life worth living. He was a fabulously wealthy man, raised high on a pedestal of power beyond measure, his name has gone down in the history books, his tomb was a great palace guarded by a great army, but still he was a poor fool, duped by his own dreams and the dizzying elevation of his position. Immortality does not exist. If you hanker after immortality, read much and walk a lot. You will not escape death, but you will live widely through the pages of books, and you will live long because walking is the slowest way of moving, so it stretches time and prolongs life. That is the best any-body can do.

The shots continue for awhile, becoming increasingly sporadic the higher we go, wasted reports in the wilder-ness, like everything that issues from the Warriors of God. Then they stop firing altogether, gather to consult. When we are almost at the top, they mount their horses and ride away. They are heading directly across the crater, not back to the southeastern cutting, but due east, presum-ably to find the easy way down the other side. They will be there, they will be looking for us, they will be waiting for us, but it does not matter, because for now we are safe and we are on top of the mountain.

At the summit, we sit in splendid isolation and gaze over the great desert to the west. The plain is mottled blue and red and brown with long mauve veins splintering from the base of the mountain like roots drawing sustenance from the bleak, beautiful landscape. It is not cold here, but without saying anything we automatically adopt that same interfolding position we enjoyed during the night above the valley of dust, Kate sat between my legs, the bone at the back of her head nestled in the indentation below my sternum, Mara bolstered by Kate's belly, head lodged between her breasts, each leaning into one another. It is like a consecration of something, something that is more precious and more soothing than anything else in life. It is hard to believe that we have been granted this 'some-thing'—I do not want to name it for fear of cheapening it or chasing it away—hard, at least, to believe that it has been granted to me. I have blood on my hands from scrab-bling among the rocks and thorny scrub, blood on my hands from the man I murdered yesterday, and yet I am at peace. Strange that one can sit on top of a mountain in perfect peace having killed a man. I cannot explain this. But it is true.

After a moment, Mara slides one hand behind her back and slips it into Kate's palm, then raises the other over her shoulder, flexing her fingers in invitation. I reach forward and clasp her hand, supporting our combined weight on one arm. We sit there for a long while, back to belly, hand in hand, watching the desert and the shifting patterns of shadow and light as they blend, then break apart shaping new patterns, so that what was clear becomes dark, and what was red becomes brown fading to beige before whitening under the light bright bleach of the wide blue sky. Then a small but welcome miracle occurs.

"Miss Kate," says Mara.

That is all—*Miss Kate*. She does not say another word, nor repeat those two words. But it is enough. She has spoken.

⊠ ⊠ ⊠

The way down is difficult, dangerous at times, but viable. The higher slopes are covered in a thick layer of fine black grit so that our descent is initially little better than an imperfectly controlled skid as we slither down sideways, legs apart, leaning back to brake the momentum, stopping when we can to kick the grit from our sandals. The gradient then eases and the grit gives way to a more stable rockslide on which we only have to look ahead and read what appears to be the easiest passage, improvising a pavement out of the largest, flattest boulders, though we can never tell for sure where each way will end, and twice have to turn back at precipitous drops, or bare rock that tapers into the wilderness of the western desert.

Despite our thirst and the hard jarring of each jump, this hopping, haphazard progress is satisfying because mind and body are so completely engaged with the landscape that we forget our weariness. It is only when we reach a broad, crimped shoulder of rock where the walking is easier that our weakness begins to show. The mountainside is a maze of interleaving crevasses and run-off channels, many leading nowhere or disappearing into one another, so it is hard to tell whether we are not deviating from our course. Time and again, we are forced to turn back from dead ends and unpromising diversions, retracing our steps until another shallow gully suggests an alternative way down, and each about turn saps our strength, until we begin to doubt there is a way out at all.

The heat is intense, thirst has gone beyond the mere discomfort of a dry mouth, becoming a kind of abstraction that disorients us even more. We do not sweat, or, if we do, it evaporates before it has time to bead and moisten the skin. Mara looks dazed, her eyes glazed with fatigue, and I carry her as much as my own intermittent dizziness will allow. The desert off to our left is no longer a thing of beauty. It has become flat and colorless in the heat and light, the immense emptiness spilling into our eyes and spinning webs of despondency in our minds. There is a dispiriting sense of going nowhere.

I try to focus my mind against the numbing emptiness, willing some significant shape into being. There may yet be a sign of previous visitors, people may have been in the habit of using this side of the mountain, and we cannot afford to miss any clue indicating a way out of here. There is nothing, though, only an endless succession of dips and rises, each rise a small incident that seems to bring us no nearer the end, and only the fact that we are still generally descending suggests we are actually getting anywhere.

Gradually, though, the dips get shallower and the shoulder levels out into a gently pitched slope of rock, scrub, and stunted trees. It is here that we see the first sign that other people have visited this place in the past. It is perhaps half a mile below us, tucked into a solitary fold, presumably the only spot where there is enough soil for it to take root. I am surprised that they grow this high. The altitude may explain why it is dead, but even a dead *tebeldi* can mean life to a traveler. The tree is ancient, stripped of bark, the branches burned away, the knot of roots exposed by erosion, but I still run forward excitedly. There is no tap hole visible in the lower bole and the main body of the tree rises high above the roots, too smooth for easy climbing, so I take out the spear and start stabbing at the trunk, trying to find a point where the wall is thin enough to breach. Mara is as excited as I am, but Kate is looking on with deep misgiving, as if I have taken leave of my senses in a large way. She has been in this country many months, but her obsession with everything that is bitter about this place has blinded her to the sweetness. I laugh a little madly, teasing her with my apparent derangement.

"Don Quijote de la Mancha!" I shout, vigorously stabbing the tree, but she doesn't get it. She watches me with the sort of regard Miss Woodhouse must have turned on Mr. Eliot when he threw himself at her in the carriage. In fact, with her wrong-headed meddling and peremptory improvement of the world at large, Kate has much in common with Emma. I keep dancing around the tree, laughing and stabbing at the naked trunk, my waistcoat flapping wildly. The heart of the tree has not been hollowed out deep, if at all, apart from the natural quarrying of insects and the elements, and I have to stab higher and higher. "Windmills! Giants! Armies!" Kate is nonplussed. Daddy may have bought her an expensive education, but she is shockingly ignorant. This is a book she needs to read. She sidles up to Mara and puts a protective arm around the child's shoulders, but Mara shrugs it off and joins me in my dance, jabbing her frail arms in the air as if she too is armed with a spear. Clearly, Kate believes our heads have been turned by the sun, that there is a lively possibility we are about to start barking, perhaps regrets not taking her chances on the plain with the Warriors of God. "Dulcinea del Toboso!" I sing, though Kate bears a better resemblance to the ingenious knight himself. All those simple moral codes overlaid on a hopelessly complex world. She really must read it. The Warriors of God could do with reading it, too. Everybody should read the bible of liberty. Except perhaps the people in government. They would be so alarmed that they would ban it straightaway.

At last, the spear finds a weak point. The tip cuts through the wood and jams in the tightly grained timber. I wait, fearing perhaps Kate's estimation of my sanity will prove accurate. But then the blade darkens and a thin, damp stripe dribbles from the wound staining the groove of the wood. The spear is too deeply embedded to come away easily, so I work it back and forth, but it is made of poor metal and the head snaps in two. I do not regret it. Despite my new awareness of what is possible, I can think of no better use for a spear. But I do not want to leave it lodged in the tree. There is every likelihood that it has been employed for less life-enhancing purposes in the past, and I do not wish to contaminate the precious liquid. The blade of the first knife also breaks, but the second is stronger, and I manage to work free the remains of the spear. Already, Mara has scrambled up the roots and is lapping at the water trickling down the trunk.

"The *tebeldi*, Miss Kate," I say, gesturing at the great gnarled roots and towering trunk, as if introducing a new and much esteemed guest. "The upside-down tree, the bottle tree, the monkey bread tree—a restaurant to dry lands." It is a kind of restaurant, too, in the proper sense of the term, a more reliable restorative than those uncertain eating places marked on the maps.

The expression on Kate's face changes as it occurs to her that this is not mere insanity, but that water is stored inside the tree. The uneasy doubt slips away, a look of wonder steals across her features, and she runs forward to join us. Now that the spear is clear, the water flows freely, and Mara presses herself to the venerable trunk, letting the liquid run over her face and into her open mouth. Kate and I briefly embrace and I find that in the simple act of folding her in my arms, of welcoming her into our delirium, I am no longer thirsty, as if I have already drunk deeply of the tree. By the time we break apart, the front of Mara's shift is soaked through and her cheeks are washed with a glistening sheen of water. I untie the blanket, hold the bucket to the gash until it is full, and pass it to Kate. I cup my hands below the cut, splash water on Mara's head, then anoint myself before drinking from the bucket. We continue like this for some minutes, drinking and rinsing away the brackish taste of bleeding gums and swollen tongues, reveling in the brief deferral of fate. There is a kind of frenzy to our drinking, almost a madness of itself, but this water is not ours to waste, so once we have drunk our fill, I stop up the hole with grit and dirt and dust, pressing it into place with the palm of my hand. The rough daub dries quickly, but there is still a trickle of water leaking from a tiny fissure at the base of the wound, which I stanch with a pellet of paper torn from a dog-eared page of *Moby Dick*. By chance, I have chosen the first page of the quotes collected by a sub-sub-librarian, the "poor devil of a Sub-Sub," a fact that, for some obscure reason, pleases me immensely. Afterwards, we sit on the shady side of the tree, enjoying the strange, deceiving sensation of being safe and free and sated.

Later, we stumble upon paradise.

◇ ◇ ◇

I say 'paradise,' but that, of course, is a personal reading of place. One of my suppliers before the war got big again was a Scottish man who had wanted all his life to live in Africa, but once here, all he did was dream of snow, of a clean white paradise to the north, and complain that we had no real seasons. It is understandable, perhaps. This is not a place of subtle shifts and muted change, and nature invariably declares itself in extremes: either it is dry or it is wet; there are no spring showers or damp autumn mornings like those described in the books; rain is torrential, never gentle, the heat heavy, rarely warm; the sky is either light or dark, there is no protracted dusk or dawn, only a sun that's suddenly there and just as suddenly gone; people are either rich or poor, not comfortably off or provided with a respectable portion; life is either peaceful or violent, hostility exploding out of nowhere without warning and disappearing again with a baffling abruptness. Little wonder that our continent attracts people of Kate's temperament looking for a platform on which to stage their dramas of good and evil, little wonder that this muggy mess of humanity makes a man dream of a cold, clean, white paradise, as pristine as anything can be in this man-struck world. But paradises are rarely cold or white. They are warm and colorful. Gold and green and silver were the colors of Jemal's paradise; it was scented with musk, which he reckoned a good thing, though neither of us had the faintest notion what musk was, let alone what it smelled like; it was decked out with fine silk and rich brocade, and pearls and other precious stones were strewn about in gaudy profusion amid the goblets and the platters, the fruit and the fowl, the couches and the thrones; and at the heart of it all lay the lovely garden with lovely ladies scrubbing his scrotum. Seventy-two of them, he said. I could tell him now that one is enough. Seventy-two, that's just plain greedy! Nonetheless, if it wasn't indefinitely postponed, his dream of paradise is not such a bad dream—*if*. I appreciate that once you have existed, non-existence is even more improbable than an afterlife, but I do not want to run the risk of waiting for a heaven that may not happen when I can chance upon some brief beauty now. Chance and transience are essential. Paradise cannot be permanent, otherwise it would only be a pretty tedium, a kind of colorful monotony, and if you try to construct it, you can be sure you will make a mess of it because paradise cannot be made, it can only be found.

It is late afternoon. We left the *tebeldi* tree about an hour ago and have been descending steadily ever since. The desert has stolen back its beauty from the setting sun and become a blaze of waves frosted with a thin fringe of pale fire. Telling sea stories, I became accustomed to seeing and describing the desert as an ocean. People need some trick of fluency or familiarity if they are to surrender to the outlandish, and though they are opposite in nature, the sea and the desert are both hostile immensities against which man is measured and made small, wildernesses that can be exploited and polluted, but not tamed. I have read of shipwrecked sailors who call the sea a desert, have heard the camel described as the ship of the desert, and know that some people die of thirst at sea while others drown in the desert, surprised by flash floods that have their origins a hundred miles away. My listeners understood the sea through the medium of the desert. This desert, in particular, backlit by the low lying sun, suggests to my imagination those wide waters I will never see except in the words of Mr. Melville, Mr. Conrad, Mr. Golding, and Mr. Hughes. There are few dunes in this quarter, but the surface of the desert is furrowed like a sheet of iron, each ripple rusted by the fast falling light of the setting sun, the dips filled with lengthening shadows, so it looks to me exactly like I imagine the sea must be, line after line of waves stretching away, the crests capped with a froth of golden light and sparkling air, as if aspiring to become another element altogether, the troughs dulled by proximity to the depths. The spectacle is so bewitching that I almost topple into paradise.

Pass fifty yards to right or left and you would miss it, so cunningly concealed is the declivity. I stop abruptly, all but tipping over the edge when the ground drops into a long green gash. Defined by a neatly pinched pleat of rock on either side, it curves away to the north, descending less steeply than the surrounding slope, so that from a distance it would resemble a narrow spine or subsidiary shoulder. The arc of the curve is such that the cavity is invisible from all sides until you actually reach the drop. From this perspective, though, it is as if we have suddenly become gods or monkeys or men in helicopters (they are all much the same only the monkeys have more humor) for the green is not the green of grass or shrubs, but of treetops. The chasm is precisely sliced into the side of the mountain, the treetops reaching the breach, but not growing above the bare rock, as if pruned to fill the gap.

Short of simply leaping in and hoping for the best, there is no access from the south, so we walk along the line of the lip, staying close to its edge, keeping the trees in view, fearing they must be a mirage in this dry place and will disappear if we stray away. They are crammed so tight, their tops so closely docked by the hot winds of the desert, that the canopy would resemble a carpet were it not for the fact that, despite the late hour, the weave is frequently breached by the flash of feathers as brightly colored birds dart in and out of the foliage. Their cries are loud and vital, giving voice to a small world of brisk life, but only audible from the very edge of the chasm, as if secretive nature has again contrived to keep this place private, swallowing the babble of birds lest they betray paradise to casual passers-by.

At its lower end, the chasm twists so sharply that it appears to be sealed, but shadowing the turn we drop down to a shallow platform where the lip doubles back like an exaggerated comma, at the tip of which there is a tiny defile, well-trodden with the tracks of baboons and jackals. Not wishing to corner a wild animal in the dark, we spend the night a few feet from the pass, but we awake at first light, eager to explore. Inside, the carpet becomes an awning, the covering of leaves so closely stitched that the sun can only penetrate at its zenith, drilling beams of bright light through fissures in the canopy that descend like solid shafts, stippling the ground with droplets of golden radiance. The bed of the chasm is even more sinuous than the lip, burrowing into the overhanging rock to form small caves and intermittent cloisters, writhing back and forth, as if some tormented wind-twisted cloud had settled in the belly of the earth, then been whipped out by a deft magician, leaving a scar as intricate and unearthly as the model around which it was molded. Toward the top, where the ground rises slightly, a hot spring breathes hazy puffs of pale vapor into the air, and a few feet below it, four rivulets of cold, clear water bubble out of the rock to feed a stream that capers along the course of the chasm, dashing down small falls and splashing through a succession of tiny pools before dipping underground again near the gateway.

Occasionally, we hear the bark of baboons and see jackals sniffing furtively around the entrance, but they never venture near. Most of the birds, however, are fearless, unaware that representatives of the world's most dangerous predator have chanced upon paradise. They carry on as if we are not there, swooping, darting, hopping, dropping, dipping, diving, ducking, a constant kaleidoscope of gleaming green, electric blue and a glossy, glassy red, their necks ringed with black collars, their backs lozenged with splashes of white, heads crowned with brown caps, eyes bespectacled with dark hoops suggesting long hours of intent study. Only two species acknowledge our presence. One is a gaily colored ground dweller, his black back spotted white, his head blotched red, the chest decorated with smudged medallions of green and gold. Like a mechanical toy, he keeps popping out of holes in the mounds of soil alongside the stream, then popping back in again as soon as he sees us, apparently endlessly surprised by our presence. The other is a kind of starling with a black head and shoulders clipped onto a chocolate breast, belly and tail, as if he has been dipped in brown dye or fought a losing battle with the polish box of a shoeshine boy. Repeatedly, he hops up, turning a stark angry eye on us, incensed that his own discrepant plumage be outdone by the coupling of a white woman with a black man. He ought to be used to such contrasts, though, for this place is profligate with color, color merged, mingled, dabbled, daubed, spattered and spread, it is everywhere, from the brilliant birds perched like bright fruit at the tops of the tallest trees to the flickering tricolor lizards flecked across the rocks like tiny flags. It is as if nature has leached all the pigments from the rest of the mountain and squeezed them into this one small fold in the rock. The trees are as extravagant as the birds, crowding together like pillars in a temple, the leaves of those I recognize larger and more abundant than any I have seen before, the branches heavy with a harvest that might feed us for months. There are kernels that can be eaten whole or steeped in water to make a dark tart drink, there is fruit filled with a nourishing pulp that can be spooned up raw or diluted to make a sweet milk, there are seeds that can be baked, nuts that poaching reduces to a porridge, buds that can be broiled, leaves that yield an aromatic potage, roots that can be roasted until they soften and emit a subtle nutty scent.

Everything is abundant, garish, overdone, which is as paradise should be, an immoderate assault on the senses. Yet the sheer licentiousness of nature does not inspire in us the sort of frenzy we felt when we found the dead *tebeldi* tree. Instead, we are hushed with wonder, walk quietly, waste no words, make no noise that might upset the magic of this other-worldly world hidden in the heart of the mountain. Mara does not speak again, as if she has said all she needs to say, but her silence no longer seems the product of horror. It is a fitting stillness mimicked by Kate and me. We do not talk, but busy ourselves gathering fruit, preparing food as complex and complete as our resources allow. On the second day, we make *merissa*. Women's work, I tell Kate, not because it is arduous, but because a woman's spit is closer to the origins of life, nearer the quick and elemental, and therefore better suited to the making of an intoxicant. I show her how to chew the *sim-sim* and *dura* till it is a mash impregnated with her saliva, then we leave it to soak, giving some to Mara in the morning before the fermentation has produced any alcohol, drinking the rest ourselves in the evening.

For all the abundance, though, it is what happens on the edges that turns this into paradise. The heart of things always lies in the margins and the idea of paradise is like a well-used book that has been annotated by successive owners until the marginalia are more important than the text that inspired them. Out on the edges, Kate and I make love. While Mara plays in the pools of water, we slip away to the chasm's more secluded corners, where we indulge in the delicious cryptology of reading bodies, noting the pauses, the punctuation, the inflections, the whole grammar of each other, writing our own comments in the borders of being. We have time to read each other, which is more than many people are allowed, and no matter how vehemently the black and brown bird may protest, the business of skin does not get between us. In the books, they always talk about the object of desire, as if desire necessarily objectifies, but Kate is no object, and desire does not reduce her to a pleasing compilation of limbs and flesh and movement, still less to a discrete component organ, no matter how accommodating that organ may be.

Only when we are spent is there some sense of reduction and then it is not the reduction of one or the other, but the senseless peace of two bodies become one.

We remain in paradise three nights and two days. I even begin to hope Kate has forgotten her memory card and the urge to remedy the irremediable. I have everything I wish for, even down to the book, albeit with a hole in it and the middle pages missing, but book enough for all that, more of a book incomplete than most other books whole. If needs be, we could hunt the baboons for meat, set snares, collect eggs, there is really no need to leave. But Kate is not one to forget, nor to forego the gratifying calumny she fancies her memory card will bring down on the Warriors of God and their distant masters in the capital. It is evening and we are drinking the *merissa* when she says thank you.

"Thank you? For the beer?"

"No," she says, "for the other day. *Is there anybody else there?* I never said thank you. Or for the nonsense in town. For everything, really."

"I think you have," I say, though she does not catch it, or chooses to ignore the implication. Perhaps lovemaking is not a matter for gratitude in her book.

"I have not behaved well. You saved me, but I've been so set on getting out and making all this public. . . ." For a few insane seconds, I almost believe she feels like me, that this paradise need not be a passing moment, that we might remain here, teasing out the thread of love to make a yarn so clean and strong that it will last forever. She pauses, then says, as if it is some great mystery that is difficult to comprehend: "But how did you know what story to tell? To make me forget my fear, I mean."

There is no mystery, though. Like most things, it was a matter of chance.

"I didn't," I say, sensing already that this talk is tending in a direction other than the one I would wish. "It was the only one that came to mind. There are many stories in the world, Miss Kate, but sometimes there is only one that can be told, and all the others are forgotten for a time."

"And one well-chosen story can save the situation?"

"It is possible. That, at least, is the way I try to save . . . situations, as you say. Through telling stories, well-chosen or otherwise."

"But you don't think my story is good enough to save this part of the world."

I touch the back of her hand. She does not respond, but neither does she withdraw. Touching is natural between us now, heedless, even when we make love it is negligent, as if this thing that is so new has been forever and will be forever, and needs no careful fostering because it exists of itself, independent of the people who express it.

"Facts, figures, a few photos are not a story, Miss Kate."

"And if they were turned into a story, would they make a difference?"

"Probably not. Even good stories do not save the world. The situation is too large."

"The attempt is still necessary, though, isn't it? Which is why we have to fight these evil people and what they are doing to your country."

Even now, though love has declared itself demanding all the customary accommodations and compromises, I am slightly irritated by her insistence on casting everything in terms of conflict and sharply contrasted opposites. It is not how she is in life. Her white skin, my black skin mean nothing to her. But in her head, the world is still black and white, still categorical, and therefore still remediable because she believes there is an unambiguous pattern for the way it ought to be. She does not openly deny the hopelessness of her need to set the world to rights, only the necessity is twisted back on itself, veering aside from the awkward obstacle of futility in order to justify side-taking, standing up, being counted, so that she may pretend we can change what no one has changed in ten thousand years. I do not mean to be unduly pessimistic, but pessimism tempered by a carefully manufactured morality might be a more practical political philosophy than any other we have produced. Too often, the belief that we can make the world better ends with the *ism*—men remodeling mankind to fit shapes they find more convenient.

I sip *merissa* from the tin cup, scoop more from the bucket and pass it to her. She drinks the muddy liquid and the foam of imperfectly mashed seeds that float on the surface leaves a gray rime along the line of her lips.

"Miss Kate, people who have their place in the world do not need to fight. The Warriors of God call men like me 'kitchen dwellers.' It is meant for an insult. They think they are free, riding across the *qoz* on their horses, declaring their liberty with their guns, that we are womanly men confined. But a kitchen dweller has his place, a place at the heart of things, beside the hearth, in the home, where food is made, and families live, and stories are told. I have my place. I do not need to fight, not like the Warriors of God, for they do not have a place in the world."

"And you think that because I want to fight it means I don't have a place in the world?"

"I do not know. But you are still looking for one. So even if you have it already, you do not know it."

I say I do not know, but I do. Her place is here with Mara and me. I reach out and trace the outline of her lips with my forefinger, wiping away the stain of the beer. She smiles, looks into my eyes with a fondness that is almost painful, but she still seems preoccupied by thoughts that have no place in our coupling, trying to make sense of things that need no sense made of them.

"If the Warriors of God and the rest of them weren't tearing everything apart, would you be happy to stay in your kitchen, in your books, undisturbed by the rest of the world?"

"Very happy. You cannot save the world, Miss Kate."

"But you have to try, don't you? Like you say, it is necessary."

For the first time, I hear doubt in her voice, a doubt that she can do anything or that anything she does will have an impact. I cannot, though, argue with my own notion that some things are necessary, however wrong-headed. At length, she says: "You have to try. I want to go on tomorrow. I want to reach Al Asher."

Thus paradise must end, this small space that I would be happy to call my place must be given up. Perhaps it is enough that we have had this. Many people never know any paradise at all or, knowing it, do not recognize it for what it is until it is too late. Perhaps it is also enough that Kate knows some small doubt, knows that not all doors can be pushed to an achievable purpose. She has learned some knowledge. It does not change how she acts, but it changes what she is. So I say: "OK, Miss Kate. Let's go and save the world, please."

Later, we lie together. We do not make love. She is on her side, tucked in the crook of my left arm, her weight tipped against me, the curve of her back tallying with my trunk as if they were modeled from matching casts. My right arm is slung across her shoulder, like a dark bandage binding her torso, while her left hand reaches back to rest on my forearm. When I move my arm down toward her hip, her hand follows, so closely that we resemble puppets pinned together to perform a dance. I brush my fingers across the furrow of her navel, which is long and deep, suggesting the cord had been tougher than is common, leaving a more pronounced scar. My hand slides lower, cradling the camber of her belly, and we stay like that, lying together, breathing together, become one for this last night in paradise.

Holding onto one another, embracing the weight of one another, these things are more important than love-making. It is the gesture, the way the paling at the out-line of my arm shades into the darkening of the shadow on her skin, the way she leans into me, a shoulder blade pressed almost painfully against the thin flesh below my collarbone. That is all there is in the end. All life is in that: a man and a woman holding onto one another on a moun-tain fearing for their lives. That is all there is.

Paradise cannot last. Paradise passes.

Is there anybody else there?

❂   ❂   ❂

Paradise has made me stupid. Perhaps that is the true nature of paradise, a weakness of mind that also dulls the senses, in this instance blunting the intuitions that have at least helped to keep us alive so far. The ambus-cade might have been foreseen. I knew there was a *wadi* not far from the foot of the mountain, had heard it was much prized among the horsemen, that it had been used in the past by the caravans because it is lined with a clay that bakes hard in the dry season, and remains imper-meable long after more friable crusts have absorbed the rainfall. There are even said to be places where pockets of moisture can be unearthed throughout the year. It was predictable that one of the roving gangs would be based there. But I did not predict it. Paradise and the unde-manding walk down the northern side of the mountain have beguiled me into a false sense of security. I knew there would be dangers out on the *qoz*. But here, so close to the mountain, so near paradise, I took no precautions, and simply lead us along the easiest line of descent, into the obvious declivity, despite the fact that there was no clear sightline to be had from it, despite the fact that it was surrounded by small outcrops of rock and hillocks of stony sand, behind which a far larger militia might have hidden. Not that it matters how many they are. Thirty men are more than enough.

Once we have walked into the trap, they rise up from their hiding places, guns trained on us. There is no escape. Stories of escape are never true. You are always caught in the end. At first, instinct tells me to react, to take out the knife, if only to provoke a fusillade that will bring things to a close more quickly, some sudden death that does not involve the incisive malice of men who must prove themselves men by cutting and penetrating. Mara has no breasts, but that will not deter them from doing what they can to unwoman a body that has yet to become the body of a woman. Kate has everything they need. Yet she is the one who stills me. Seeing me tense, perhaps leaning to move, she says, "No, don't." I hesitate and the moment is gone, because they have reached us and taken hold of Kate, so there will be no sudden end. Kate with her imperishable optimism, the faith that there is no such thing as a time when all is lost, hopes that there is some way out of this, that so long as we survive, there is a chance.

They are not Warriors of God. Some are dressed in the manner, with the white robes and the long cloths wound about their heads to protect them from the sun, but most are in a motley collection of military camouflage and western-style civilian clothes, and they have no horses. Above all, they are dark-skinned, so it is unlikely that they are employed by the government. It does not matter who employs them, though, nor what motive they have found in faith or politics or pocket, because all men with guns, whatever they may protest, are made in the same image. They order us to take off our clothes. It is starting. The butchery is about to begin. Kate cannot forget, but I doubt she remembers with more acute anguish than I do.

Again I waver, not fearing what is about to be done to me, but wondering whether there is anything I can do to prevent what is about to be done to them. The hesitation is enough to provoke our captors. Something hard hits me from behind, a glancing blow across the back of the head. Consciousness is not lost, though. I am knocked out briefly, but consciousness returns all too soon. It is not something you can dispense with so easily when you wish. Apart from the ache where I have been clubbed, there is no pain when I come to, no blood, no dismemberment. Mara is held by two boys barely older than herself. She is naked, shivering in the midday heat, her body thin and brittle, built more like a bicycle than a girl. I had not noticed it in paradise when she was cavorting in the water, as if joy had lent flesh to her bones. But here she looks unbearably fragile, like those blue butterflies in the valley of dust, something alive that logic tells you should be dead. Kate has been stripped as well, but she is not trembling, nor crouching clutching her belly or face as I had feared. There is no blood and she is standing as normally as a naked woman can among a gang of armed men. She looks scared, but less than I would wish. I do not know what these particular men believe, but men with guns, any men with guns anywhere in the world, do not take kindly to women who can stand before them, stripped naked, and not cower at their power. I am kicked, told to move, kicked again until I stand. Our belongings are sifted, mostly discarded. The knife has been taken with my clothes.

Prodded by the guns, we walk for about a mile until we reach the *wadi* at a point where it is wide enough to hold a large encampment. There is no standing water, but there must be a source nearby. There are a dozen more men, plus a truck, and several jeeps and pickups. The vehicles are dented and ancient, among them a Landrover I recall doing the run between Anahud and Al Asher. It must be at least forty years old, was already notorious a decade ago when it regularly broke down, obliging passengers to walk till they were picked up by a truck; but in this war nothing is too old or too young to be pressed into service. We are not presented to any leader, nothing is asked of us, and nothing is given. We are simply pushed into a small wooden cage that has been cobbled together from strips of plastic, a couple of saplings, and an assortment of old planks. It is too low for Kate and me to stand in, so we squat on the crossbars that make up the floor, watched by a boy who must be Mara's age if not younger. He has hooded eyes and a gun almost as tall as himself that he handles negligently, as if it is a natural extension of his slender, long-fingered hands.

Come nightfall, a score or so of the company climb into the jeeps and drive into the desert. They do not turn on the vehicles' headlights. For all I know, the lights may be broken, but it is more likely that, wherever they are going and whatever they are doing, they do not want to be seen. The child still stands guard, apparently used to long, unrelieved shifts. Occasionally, he leans against a rock and dozes. It is the only time we can speak. When he is awake and we talk, he silences us with an angry, frightened wave of the oversized gun.

"They're black," whispers Kate.

"Yes, Miss Kate, I had noticed. Top marks."

"Don't be fucking flippant," she hisses. At any other time, it is a concept that might please me, fucking flippancy, a sort of levity of lovemaking; but the fact of what will probably happen to her makes any idea of lovemaking too painful. "It means they're against the government, doesn't it?"

"Probably."

"Well, they might help us."

For all her fighting, Kate does not understand about men with guns and their sorry need for a little control. Even if her mad plan were to have any impact in the wider world, even if they could be persuaded the wider world would be against the interests of their enemies, I doubt these men would want to help her. Why invite the intervention of the wider world, which has many more guns than they do, when they already enjoy the illusion of some little power without the wider world interfering? But Kate is adamant, we must try, it is necessary, and I promise to ask the boy what group they belong to.

When, at length, he wakes, he is little inclined to talk, and it takes me some time to work out what language he speaks. Eventually, though, we find common words and he tells me they are the JMD. I have never heard of them, ask him what the letters stand for, but he does not know. He is just a child who has been taken from his village and given a gun, a child who has learned to do what he is told and ask no questions. When I tell this to Kate, tell her we can only wait and hope to see someone in authority, the boy is alarmed by the strange words, and starts waving the gun again.

There really is nothing to do but wait. Whoever the JMD are, they will declare themselves sooner or later. It is enough that nothing worse has happened than being stripped naked and put in a cage. I would guess they are just one more bunch of bandits who hope an acronym will lend their activities a semblance of political legitimacy, bandits who have got lucky in the seizing of a foreigner, and are trying to work out what benefit can be gained from it. Sometimes I think there must be an equation relating the proliferation of acronyms to the mess we are making of the world, because you can be sure that the more of them there are, the more likely it is that there will be people suffering nearby. I still haven't worked out whether the Warriors of God are irredeemably dim or their name is a cunning ruse to discourage the sensitive western media from discussing their activities.

Though milder than on the mountain, the night air is still too cold for being outside without clothes or shelter;

so the three of us huddle in a corner of the cage, not as we did on the mountain, but side by side with Mara in the middle, in a vain attempt to stay warm. Despite the desperate situation, there is something comforting in our attitude, something about Kate and I shielding Mara that does not exactly give hope, but at least defies despair. No matter how difficult life becomes, no matter how likely it is that life will end shortly, there is an animal warmth to community, an emotional comfort that even the cold cannot eclipse. Perhaps it is this that makes Africa so appealing to people like Kate, not just the drama of a land that lends itself to their piebald morality, but the sense of a place that has not become atomized like the mon-eyed world they come from, a place where people are not just individuals, each responsible for himself and him-self alone, but where community still counts like it used to count in the books of Miss Austen and Mrs. Gaskell. I do not properly understand what has happened out there in the rich countries, have only deduced what I can from chance meetings, radio reports, and the occasional modern novel; but it reads like a world where happiness is defined by anything apart from the simple, age-old plea-sure of belonging. In Africa, the world at large discovers a memory of what it once was and regrets it will never be again. In Africa there is no well-being without community. Even the Warriors of God understand that. Everything is community, even three people huddled in a cage on the edge of the desert, and the being together is enough to lull us into a fitful sleep that lasts almost till dawn.

※　※　※

The boy may not know what JMD stands for, but what-ever it is, he knows he does not want to die for it or go out of his way to make other people die for it, because as soon as the first shots are fired, he is up and off and sprinting in the opposite direction.

It is dark in the *wadi*. The only illumination comes from a small fire in the middle of the camp. By its light, I can make out running figures, men on horseback, white robes, the dull gleam of the remaining vehicles. A man in army fatigues dashes across the face of the fire before being cut down by a horseman. Sound disperses itself into a sporadic rat-a-tat-tat of shouts, screams, gunshots, and drumming hooves. Two men on horseback gallop past the cage without noticing us. An engine fires, misfires, then goes quiet. There is a scuffle on the far side of the camp, the noise of hard things hitting hard things, a man's voice, angry and defiant, then suddenly begging for mercy, briefly before going quiet like the motor. The shooting continues, comes in waves that shift from one quarter of the camp to another. The horsemen gallop back again, still not noticing us. I notice them, though. I know them. They are Warriors of God.

The main bars of the cage are thick and will not break, but the framework is only roughly bound together with old bits of string and strips of rubber cut from a petrified inner tube. When I stand, the top section reaches midway down my back. Not for the first time, nor the last, I am grateful for the strength given by books. I brace my feet on the floor struts and push upward. The wooden bars give slightly and I fear they are too flexible, but suddenly the bindings in one corner crack so that the top of the cage can be pushed back slightly. The gap is too small to get through, though. I shift to the opposite corner, brace my feet, push again. An old plank breaks, but there is enough leverage to keep pressing till several more bindings snap.

Then I hear my name. A man's voice. There is still a confusion of sounds, still many horses galloping, men shouting, shots being fired, but that voice carries because it is a voice I know well. Jemal is twenty yards away, alone for the moment while his men continue to pick off the remaining members of the JMD. He is on foot. There is no sign of the Landcruiser, but he carries a short whip, like the horsemen sometimes use when riding. I cannot clearly see his expression, but his face is set in a manner that suggests coldness, and I have the impression he is smiling. The time has come. Jemal is going to kill me. Perhaps he has hit upon his own paradise in the shape of such unexpected luck, chancing on a prey he must have thought long lost. For my part, I have only one wish now. I want him to shoot Kate and Mara first to save them from what his men will do otherwise. I think it is his men, too, not him. I do not believe, or rather, would not believe that the boy who spoke so warmly of maidens with swelling breasts can bring himself to cut away the sex of a woman, even one deemed immoral by the code they have conjured up to justify their cruelty. But it makes no difference. The work will be done one way or another unless I can persuade him to kill them first.

Kate has other ideas, though. Kate always does. While I stand petrified in one corner of the cage, mesmerized by the sight of my former friend, calculating whether I can make any claim on the friendship for the sake of my companions, she is trying to eat her way out. At first, I do not understand what she is doing. She has pressed her face into the far corner of the cage and appears to be chewing at the bars. Jemal seems perplexed, too, staring at her, probably wondering like me whether she has not completely lost her head. But Kate is sharper than us. She has seen that there is only one binding keeping that side of the cage closed, and she is set upon biting through it.

It gives, she steps back with bloodied mouth, lifts her arms and flips the top of the cage open. Jemal and I act as one. He starts running, I start rocking. We will not have time to clamber out before he reaches us, certainly Mara won't, but with the second hard shove of my shoulders I manage to topple the cage. At the same instant, a bullet tears through the base bars sending splinters of wood into my thigh. There is a moment's confusion before we extricate ourselves, then Kate and I are clear, and are scrabbling on all fours to distance ourselves from Jemal. It is too late, though. He has already circled the cage, is standing in front of the open end, his revolver leveled on Kate. I am so relieved that I almost want to thank him. He thinks to punish me by killing her first, seeing in our nakedness some sign of an intimacy at which he could otherwise only guess. He does not understand that he is doing me a favor. I can stand dying, but dying with the thought of what is to be done to Kate and Mara afterwards, that would be intolerable. Except something is missing, both from Jemal's calculation and my relief. Mara is only just emerging from the cage.

I don't know where she learned about such things. Such a quiet child, too.

Jemal shrieks with anguish. The prospect of lovely ladies wafting their swelling breasts about and sponging away at his private parts for all eternity was really very pleasing. Having Mara crawl up behind him, reach between his legs, and squeeze his genitals, very, very hard indeed by the sound of things, is another matter altogether. The gun goes off, but fires wide, and in the next instant my head hits his chest. It is not very elegant, even by the standards of a head-butt, but in the circumstances it will do. Jemal is knocked clean over the top of Mara and into the cage. I grab her, double her over my shoulder like a sack, and start running, Kate at my side. We are at the end of our wits, we have spent every last reserve of ingenuity and energy; we are tired, hungry, cold and thirsty, we are naked and running into a wilderness without any provisions or means of surviving, we are hunted and have no real hope of escaping men on horseback, but for the moment we are together and we are free. As for Jemal, he is doing as well as can be expected.

❈ ❈ ❈

We hurry across the *qoz*, moving to stay warm, moving to get away, moving because there is nothing else to do except hide or die, only there is nowhere to hide, and Kate has already expressed a disinclination to die. The moon-dark, star-bright sky stands about us like a large black bell studded with diamonds, a sheltering dome that will shield us for another hour. Twice, we hear horses, flatten ourselves against the ground, though there is little risk of being discovered in the dark. Otherwise, we keep moving, ignoring the stones and thorns that bruise and prick our bare feet, walking through the night, heading northeast as best I can judge, toward the crossroads, the well of books, and the road to Al Asher.

With the rising of the sun, we are brought back to the familiar dangers of the low lying morning light. It is perhaps the story of my life, standing out against the horizon, showing the shape of a man, a shape that provokes those who prefer the shadow play of God. I used to hide in books, enjoying that peculiar invisibility they lend, but now I suspect my books also formed a kind of horizon against which I was silhouetted, making me a target for the likes of Fr. Gianni and Jemal, men of such sour failure and rickety spirit that they cannot endure the idea that there are other worlds where life may be wider, brighter, larger, and louder than the life they are capable of living, most especially worlds conjured from the imagination and a few marks on a page. Books always scare men like them who covet power, particularly when their hold on power is uncertain or premised on violence. Would Jemal have pursued us so relentlessly if something of this nature had not made me stand out strong in his life? I still do not know. Perhaps the recollection of my scorn for the spotless pudenda of paradise is provocation enough. Perhaps it was the shock of shooting someone who then got up and walked away. Perhaps it is Kate and her memory card. Doubtless the startling violence done to his testicles is an aggravating factor. But whatever the cause, he and his men keep coming after us.

About an hour after sunrise, we see a curl of dust kicked up by a vehicle to the west, and catch sight of several figures in white dotted across the *qoz* half a mile behind us. Later, we hear distant gunfire. At one point, the helicopter is audible, but so far away we cannot see it. Then a group of horsemen appears to the southeast, riding parallel to us. They have not seen us, but they are looking, and they have understood the way we must go. Jemal knows the only place we can hope to get help, knows also that we cannot get far without food or water or clothes. It might have been wiser to return to paradise, but I am not sure we would have found it again. Once you have left, you cannot go back to paradise. You have just got to keep moving.

So we keep on keeping on, dodging as best we can between the poor shelter of shallow rises, and occasionally lying flat when a group of horsemen come near enough to see us. We hear the helicopter for a second time about mid-morning, but still cannot make out where it is. Eventually, we reach the first rutted tracks of the swathe of trails that constitute the road to Al Asher, many churned so deep that the surface grit is streaked with the sandy yellow loam that lies underneath. The crossroads is half a mile to the north, a few hundred feet before the well of books. There used to be a small settlement here that served as a truck stop, but the people have long since been chased away, and the shacks are collapsing back into the ground from which they were made. It is the way we are prone to go, too. We cannot carry on like this. Even without the Warriors of God hunting us, Al Asher is too far, we are too weak, worn out by the frantic flight and the fatigue engendered by fear, cold, heat, and hunger. Our best chance is to hide and hope a peacekeeping convoy will pass, or at least a merchant's truck, though whether anyone would stop for three naked figures reeling out of the wilderness, I do not know. Given what is going on here, stopping for strangers is not advisable. The only place to hide is the well of books.

The hole is much as it was last time I came. A couple of bricks have broken away from the lip and slipped in among the books, but the interior walls are sound, and even Mara has no difficulty climbing down the ten feet or so to the bottom. Some of the stock is damaged, though. Vermin have eaten through the plastic and several books are wet from the recent rain. We suck the moisture from the damp pages. It helps a little, but there is no pretending we are anything but at the limits of endurance. It is over a day since we ate, longer since we drank. We will probably die here. So long as we do not show ourselves above ground, it is unlikely that the Warriors of God will find us, but equally unlikely that anyone will pass before hunger and thirst finish us off. Venturing out, I might trap the odd rodent, gather grasses or edible bark, we could even eat the books, but there is no water here. The vulture knows it, too.

I first see him in the early afternoon. He is circling high above us, very high, not threatening, just watching, interested, like a collector's agent who sees the harvest fail, and knows that in due course the country people will be forced to sell their family totems and ancestral devices. I pay no attention. I have been shadowed by vultures in the past. They are graceless creatures that get their living as best they can, not so very different from the rest of us; for though this world best rewards the predators, most of us are scavengers, scrabbling about to see what we can pick up from the leavings of the bigger beasts. Vultures are very human creatures. Perhaps that is why they have such a bad reputation. But then I realize what this particular vulture signifies. Vultures have watched me in the past, waiting to see how weak I would become, but never when I was being pursued by the Warriors of God. If Jemal's men happen to look up, if they see the vulture, they will know where to find us. I start moving vigorously around the pit, climb its walls, check nobody is in sight, then stroll around, jumping and hopping, essaying a little dance of life. Kate, who is so exhausted that she can barely bring herself to move, regards me as if I have again taken leave of my senses. But there are no bookish jokes this time. The vulture seems to make the same evaluation of both my efforts and my wits. He will not be discouraged by a poor display of vitality. He knows what is going on down here. He can afford to wait.

An hour later, I clamber up for perhaps the fifth time and peer over the edge. This time, the horsemen are visible. They are heading toward us, around fifty of them in all, side by side in an irregular line. The bird still circles, knowing it cannot land yet, but meditating on the prospect, calculating the risks and rewards, thinking the time will come, that it only has to be patient, that with a little help from the Warriors of God its hovering expectancy will become a self-fulfilling prophecy. I duck down, wait a few minutes, then raise my head again. They are coming on, steady, not hurrying, trotting toward us. Jemal is on horseback in the center of the line. Though ragged, the formation is such that it is impossible for them to miss us. The only hope is that they might change direction once they reach the main traces at the crossroads. For the present, they are simply traversing the *qoz*. But maybe they are making for the main trails. Maybe. That is the great weakness of readers, the point at which we become fallible:

we are too caught up with maybes, all the possible things that can happen in all the possible lives that can be lived, so that in the end we are as incorrigibly optimistic as a can-do Kate. In this case though, the maybe is soon dashed. One of the men near Jemal points at the sky. He has seen the vulture. They move no faster, but keep coming on, and there is no hope they are going to turn aside before they reach us.

There is only one more maybe. I slither over the rim of the well, keeping low to the ground, and crawl toward the crossroads. If I can get far enough away before they find me, maybe they will be satisfied with my blood, and will not bother hunting down Kate and Mara. It is improbable, I know. After the mistreatment of his genitals last night, Jemal will want every revenge he can get, especially against the sex that unmanned him. Even if he does not, their deaths will not be easy, cracking up in the heat, their only respite the too cold nights, waiting for the wild animals to sense a critical infirmity. But perhaps I can save them from the business of the lips above and the lips below.

The Warriors of God are several hundred yards short of the crossroads when I show myself on the nearside. Jemal raises an arm to halt his men. The horses directly in front of me prance sideways, startled by the unexpected apparition of a figure rising out of the earth. Jemal calms his horse, urges it forward. His men remain where they are, still lined up, as if awaiting a starter's gun. This is no race, though. They have all the time they need. They believe themselves immortal, after all. They wait and watch. It is understood. This is a personal quarrel between Jemal and me.

Another maybe. If I can get to him, can get at him, can unseat him, can kill him, maybe the rest will be so disconcerted that they will run away. All I need is momentum to keep me going. There is no sign of the revolver yet, though I do not doubt that he is armed. He may have God on his side, but even he is unlikely to rely entirely on the uncertain assistance of divine intervention. He will have his gun, a dagger, too, possibly other metal items deemed appropriate expressions of celestial license. Let him shoot me, his bullets will not stop me, let him stab and kick and cut and club and batter. I will not be broken, not yet. I am going to kill him. You do what you have to in order to survive. Nothing more, nothing less.

I start running, imagining that all my books are on my back, not weighing me down but driving me forward with the power of all the words and all the imagination they contain. Jemal prods his horse so that it trots toward me. I race at him, remembering the whale, that a loose fish no matter how badly wounded can still unseat man and all his cracked ways. Jemal stands briefly in his stirrups, a loose fish in his own sense, floating fearfully in waters too wide and deep for comprehension, tossed about by currents that will not claim or sustain him, grasping at God for fear of sinking under the surface. He shouts his faith in a deity that would quail to see what is done in His name, drops back into the saddle, and spurs the horse into an easy gallop. I shout back, quoting my own faith, that there is an ungraspable phantom in life, a universal thump that is passed around, that all hands should rub each others' shoulder blades, and be content, because we all feel the clout sooner or later, and there is no purpose or value to life if we do not try to ease one another's pain.

But Jemal does not care for the vaporings of a smuggling verbalist. Loose fish and fast fish and universal thumps are nothing to him, and Herman is a name that would at best bring to mind the insufferable image of an hermaphrodite. He does not listen. Instead he rides with his hands held high, as if surrendering, the horse's reins draped across the pommel of the saddle. His fingers are spread wide, the thumbs at right angles to the forefingers, and he is showing me his palms, because he believes that the number of the beautiful names is written in the lines of his hands, and that in showing me the number, he can invoke God and break me before bullet and blade are brought to bear. Like the verses in the amulet, it is his faith, his charm, his trick.

"Barkis and Peggotty, Pip and Estella, and Jim and Della," I recite, gasping short, sharp, shallow breaths that swallow the names. I am worn out, stumbling and mumbling like a somnambulist, but still I will recite the loves of a life well-read. These are my beautiful names and, though Jemal will not hear them, it is only fit that I give voice to another, less ugly faith. "Emma and Knightley, Margaret and John, Jane and Rochester; Madeline and Gussie, Darcy and Lizzie, Joseph and Fanny; David and Catriona, the Don and Dulcinea, Will and Dorothea, Tom and Sophia. . . ."

I do not believe as Jemal believes that names and charms can influence the outcome of a confrontation with death. Beautiful names, be they of God or books or both, are a construct, we conjure them for the sake of good companions and a necessary escape into the happiness of imaginary worlds. But if battle must be done, it is best done with beautiful names in one's mouth.

"Queequeg, Tashtego, and Dagoo; Jaggers, Wemmick, and Pocket; Booby, Adams, and Wilson; Stubb, Starbuck, and Flask; Micawber, Traddles, and Dick; Bildad, Charity, and Peleg; Jim, Huck, and Tom . . ."

Jemal lowers his hands, dips toward the horse's withers, snatches up the reins, straightens in the saddle, draws his revolver, and raises the barrel.

Run, books, run! Run me on, run me through the weapons of warriors and the hopelessness of hope, run me through the beautiful names.

"*Oliver Twist, Nicholas Nickleby, Our Mutual Friend*; Kipps, Kim, and Emma; *Pride and Prejudice, Sense and Sensibility*; *Wuthering Heights, Bartleby, the Scrivener, Tom*

Sawyer, *Ivanhoe* and *The Black Arrow*; *The History of Mr. Polly* . . ."

Jemal is not aiming at me, though. The gun is level, pointing too high for the chest of this particular, long-cherished target. It is trained on something behind and beyond me, as if the greater threat is the threat further away. I glance over my shoulder. Kate is running hard, running to catch up, to overtake, to take control, to save the world wherever she can, running with an energy that denies her spent reserves. Watching her run and wondering that the will can overthrow the weakness of the body, I trip on a stone, have to run harder to keep from falling. Jemal fires. My running cannot keep up with my falling and I hit the ground, turning on the instant to see what has happened. Kate has fallen, too. The horse is nearly upon us, snorting and stamping. Jemal can barely master the beast. Kate rises, staggers, goes down on one knee. There is blood on her right leg, an ugly wound in the thigh. Jemal is forcing his horse around in order to fire at me. I am getting to my feet, but too slow, far too slow. A whirling shape of naked flesh tumbles toward the horse's hooves. Kate has thrown herself forward so that she is between Jemal and me. She is rolling over and over, rolling at the horse. Unlike its rider, the animal is not schooled to trample on the living. Its tastes are too nice to match the cruel ways of men. It shies, rears, veers away. I rush in before Jemal can wrestle back control. Kate is curled in a small ball, her hands raised to protect her head.

I reach up, get my arms around Jemal's waist, and drag him from the saddle. He thrashes in my arms like a landed fish. There is a flash of a blade, a gout of blood, but I do not feel anything. I get one hand around the nape of his neck, grasp the waistband of his trousers with the other, and heave him high above my head. We stall a moment, quiver as one, almost like lovers shuddering together in a moment of ecstasy, then I hurl him at the ground with all the weight of all the books I have read and carried about on my back and in my head and in my bones, so that it is as if the books themselves are beating him back into the earth. The horse gallops away. Jemal groans, tries to turn, sighs, lies still. I look back toward the well of books. Mara has not shown herself and I catch myself thanking God, somebody's God, anybody's God for that small mercy. I help Kate to her feet. The Warriors of God are moving. But they are not riding away from us. One man down is not enough. They are riding at us. They have guns in their hands and God in their hearts. And we are standing at the crossroads.

I must find Jemal's gun. But when I let go of Kate, she sinks to the ground, unable to support her own weight. I turn back, kneel beside her. There is no point, anyway. We are lost, there is no escape. It is over. In the end, not even Kate can stand on her own, and I am not going to leave her for the sake of some infantile act of defiance. This is it, the universal thump, it comes to us all, and there is nothing to do but hold one another and share the blows. I am whimpering, perhaps even blubbering like a baby, because I know what is left, I know what is going to happen now. The Warriors of God are coming and they are going to take Kate away, take my Kate, and take from her that which frightens them most.

I reach out and wrap her in my arms, strong arms, big shoulders.

I will not let it happen.

I hold her tight, whisper words of love in her ear, then put my arms around her head. I place a hand across her face, pinch shut her nostrils, press hard on her mouth, squeezing her lips till they are firmly closed, and hold her tight, tight with all the love and desolation I know. Despite the violence, she takes it for a gesture of love, which it is, and she leans into me, as if to aid in the stifling of a life that is still capable of suffering. I have my back to the Warriors of God, can ignore them safely because they cannot hurt me anymore, and I will not allow them to hurt Kate. This is the quick of it, the moment when it is stilled, the consummation if you like, not a conventional loving but a loving nonetheless, because it is ready to kill everything it cares for in order to care for that thing and save it from pain.

It is not pretty, her small face mashed in my large hand like that, it is not pretty, the purpose of this love that lends strength to my arms, but at such a pass as this, it is the nearest thing to beauty we are allowed. The gesture is ugly and the slender delicacy of the sentiment is destroyed by its realization, but there is something in it of selflessness. That the self will be less, I know for sure. I can already feel it emptying, everything I care about receding into the past, the tricks that have kept me going leaking away with the waning of the life in my hands. No more books, no more stories, no more necessary beliefs, just this, the end. At least she seems to understand that the killing is mutual, that I am also suffocating myself by this act. *I took her hand in mine, and we went out of the ruined place; and, as the morning mists had risen long ago when I first left the forge, so, the evening mists were rising now, and in all the broad expanse of tranquil light they showed to me, I saw no shadow of another parting from her.* That is the way. No shadow of another parting. We are walking out of this ruined place together, leaving behind the dust and rancor, walking into the evening mists.

It is a walk too far, though. She starts to struggle. I wish the expanse of tranquil light had continued to grow, getting broader and broader until it became so big and bright that it collapsed back into darkness. If the stillness could have come quietly, a curtain descending softly to eclipse the light. But some instinct to survive to the very end gives the lie to my act of love. Her chest is heaving and she is trying to twist away from me. I hold her close, dare not look in her eyes, keep whispering all the loving-kindness I know, knowing it is not enough, but knowing that this at least is something I can do for her. I cannot save her. Nobody can save anyone or anything, least of all the world. But I can save her from the bloody business of the lips. If only she would understand. Perhaps she does. But her body will not give in, keeps kicking and struggling in its ignorant need to know a few more seconds of life.

She is weakening, I can feel it in my hands, yet still she continues to resist, a shoulder turned against my chest, the good leg pushing against the ground. It hurts. The blade of her bone has lodged itself between my ribs, is digging into my heart, hard and fast, as if to stick itself there for evermore. But for all the hurt, I hold on because there is nothing else to do. Her hands clasp my forearm, a wretched parody of our last night in paradise that makes me think this is hell. Her body bucks slightly, goes rigid with panic or a final spasm of effort, but she has no strength, nothing to measure against the weight of all those books built up in my arms and shoulders. I do not see the Warriors of God. They are no longer relevant. All that matters is all the love I can squeeze into squeezing the life out of my love.

Sometimes circumstances make us kill the one we love.

Sometimes circumstances kill the one we love.

Sometimes circumstances make us kill love.

Sometimes circumstances kill love.

I still cannot get this right, even now.

Then the Warriors of God reach us. But they are too late. Cheating myself, I have cheated them, too.

She is still.

It is done.

Kate is dead.

No shadow of another parting.

They are all around us, dismounting, dragging us apart, enraged at being deprived of their sport. They are kicking, punching, clubbing, but not killing, not yet. I am the killer. For love, I have killed my love.

I glimpse the dark glint of a dagger, but it does not matter, nothing matters, I do not struggle. The blade nicks the back of my knee, saws back and forth sundering the ligament. There is pain, I am almost glad of it, but it is not enough, it is nothing beside the pain of what I have done for love. If ever there was a God, I would pray to Him now. Let them excise the rest, let them cut away the flesh that shared the flesh of Kate, let them amputate the hands that held her, pluck out the eyes that saw her, tear out the tongue that tasted her, let them dig out the soul, that fifth wheel to a wagon, for it is dead and done with, and only needs burying to keep the world a little tidy.

But I am not to be granted that.

There are worse things than dying. One of them is to survive when love is dead, above all when it has been killed by one's own hand.

It comes in waves, hard by, the only god we know, the rush of air, a racket of dust and dead grass and the clatter of man's crazed ingenuity, the universal thump that serves us all, the *whomp-a-whomp-a-whomp* hopelessly holding up hope in the midst of despair.

I whisper love in her ear, but she does not hear.

She is still. It is done. Kate is dead.

And we are standing at the crossroads.

❂   ❂   ❂

Unknotting. Apart from escape, this is the most misleading fabrication of the stories we tell ourselves, the idea that there can be an unraveling of events that makes everything clear and comprehensible. It is a necessary deception, but real stories end in doubt, the holes patched up with conjecture. For what it is worth, here are the facts. Kate would have been proud of me. Except that the facts are seeded with lies.

Her body was transported to the capital and repatriated with all her belongings. There, one fact, and already a lie is embedded in it. Naked women fleeing through the desert have no belongings. Yet Kate went home with items very like those she had intended taking, pictures of the atrocities that have been committed here, pictures consecrated by her martyrdom, and which had more impact than I had believed possible. Who planted them on her, I do not know, but they went around the world, briefly causing the outcry she had anticipated if not the consequences. She had expected protests, sanctions, intervention. Instead, the government declared the entire region too dangerous for foreigners and expelled all non-nationals. Even the peacekeepers and those charities that had stayed in Al Asher were obliged to leave. Her message was willfully misread, became not a cause for engagement, but a pretext for disengagement. Worse, I believe it may have facilitated what she had hoped to stop. I am far away now, in a city in another country, but occasionally refugees reach this remote place, and their accounts suggest the clearance of people continues on an even larger scale; that the marriage of money and politics which Kate claimed had aggravated the old conflicts is still doing the work it needs to do, or the work is being done for it, only now unhampered by any outside witnesses.

Our most cherished beliefs about ourselves are often the most wrongheaded, what we believe to be our strengths, actually our weaknesses. Kate thought she was a strong independent woman righting wrongs. At my lowest moments, I fear she was a hapless tool in the making of more wrong. The gap between what we want to be and what we become is perhaps even greater when we are actively engaged with the world, trying to make things better by pointing out where they have gone wrong.

Presenting ourselves and our aspirations, we are like glass grinders making lenses: our purpose is to make the world clearer, but what others see through those lenses depends on how they are held and what they are applied to. Kate wanted people to react, but instead they have accepted the government's interdiction and have retreated, repelled by images of a nation of victims, of non-people that may be pitied but not respected, only too ready to ignore what is happening. There is the myth of Kate, of course, the story that so excited the media, but that has nothing to do with this place, everything to do with another place that feels it has lost its way, and no longer knows how to invoke ideals. They have taken the lens of her life and turned it on themselves.

Why we were hunted, how they knew what Kate intended, if indeed they did know, remains a mystery. Even Sadiq, who was so garrulous on other subjects, would not tell me. I suppose it is possible, as Kate suggested, that her call was intercepted (I know nothing about such things and care less), that the Warriors of God were set on our trail, that someone then decided better use could be made of an idealistic foreigner, and the helicopter was sent to find us first. Sheer bad luck might provide an equally plausible explanation, though. The authorities may simply have been making the best of a bad job, the Warriors of God could as easily have been operating on their own. Certainly, it has long been known that the control the government exercises on these groups is very imperfect, that guns, once given, create their own logic, and that the men in power and their henchmen would readily dispense with one another if it was reckoned expedient. Jemal was most definitely dispensed with. He was accused of killing Kate and hanged for the crime, credited with what he had wanted and failed to do. Again, pictures were published, grainy images of the hooded body hanging from a scaffold, heavy and limp, and looking very unlike the sort of lively young lad liable to have lovely ladies clambering all over his lap. Sadiq showed me the national newspaper with the photograph on the front page. Told me, too, that Jemal was already dead when they reached us, his back broken by the weight of books behind my arms. He appeared to find it funny that they had 'executed' a dead man. To me, it seems fitting that a government whose primary concern is holding onto power should need to kill a corpse. Sham is as vital to bullies as brutality.

The story did not stop there, though. Several foreign papers picked up on Kate's personal history, the lone woman with a mission, traveling on her own in hostile territory to expose a scandal. That the scandal was soon forgotten was not important. All that mattered was the image of an idealist in danger. That was the juice of the matter because idealism has otherwise been lost in those countries and they can only resuscitate its ghost by telling themselves stories of great deeds in distant places. As for Mara and me, we were never there. Africans are always written out of their own story. Our purpose is to illustrate the extremities of life, to provide pictures of heartrending drama and a backdrop of darkness against which the world may set its morality play. We are victims on the sidelines, never central players. Personally, it does not trouble me. I do not mind being written out of my story with Kate—it is still my story, the version promoted abroad somebody else's story. From what I understand, a kind of cult has developed about this idealistic young woman who died so tragically, a book has been written tracing her progress from privilege to activism, there is even talk of a film. It is not a book I will read, nor a film I will see. I only have time for what is true.

I will not tell you how I felt when I woke in the military clinic and realized I was still alive. Suffice to say that I believe I would have willed myself to death if they had not told me I had a daughter. It was Sadiq who informed me.

He is a type often seen in the towns that were previously visited by foreign journalists and diplomats, one of those smooth, educated men employed by the government to give a smooth, educated face to a regime that is otherwise brutal and stupid, a specialist in nimble promises and sluggish practices. When the helicopter landed, Mara had her arms about my neck, was trying to shield me from the Warriors of God with her own body. It touched his heart, he said, indicating that organ with more certainty as to its whereabouts than I would have dared display in his shoes. He has a daughter about her age, he said. He liked to think that in similar circumstances . . . The sentiment of monsters, except there are no monsters, only more or less ordinary people who are prepared in certain situations to do things we describe as monstrous—like I have done. It seems it is my fate to be saved by women: by Jenny's books, by Mihad's sex, by Kate throwing herself in front of Jemal's horse, by the devotion of Mara. If Sadiq hadn't suffered that spasm of tender feeling, I would have been killed, for I could serve no purpose in the plot that was being elaborated, unless the one subsequently assigned to Jemal. It would have been more just, even if the proper ascription of blame would not have made the story any more true. Only the accident of being found by a lonely father pining for his family and, perhaps, who knows, wearied by all the killing, saved me from the Warriors of God. Like Queequeg's coffin, Mara bobbed out of the whirlpool and has become a life buoy on which I float, an orphan for an orphan, a Rachel for an Ishmael.

She is at my side now. She still does not speak except in the written words I am teaching her. It is the greatest gift I can offer. Reading is a rite of passage, a gateway into the adult world, and a means of accessing what went before, what has become, and what will be. Writing is its complement, another way of participating in the dialogue between past, present and future. Perhaps one day, she will record her own story, or perhaps her story will only exist in these pages. Either way, this text is for her. What she does with it, she must decide. Along with the words I am giving her, it will be my only legacy, for I will not grow rich from my work as a public scribe. Sadiq offered to send us south to one of the safe camps across the border, but I preferred to go west, lighting out for the territories, into the heart of the continent and a country even more obscure in world affairs than my own. They left us at the frontier, where the great desert shades into grass, and watched as we walked away into another land, Mara supporting me by my elbow while I hobbled along, reduced by the unfamiliar crutches to a shambling quadruped.

I no longer walk or read, though I am not so crippled that I cannot shift myself about as required. For the most part, though, I sit in the marketplace next to the post office with Mara at my side, teaching her words and waiting for small commissions. I sit and write, other people's words, other people's letters, other people's lives, other people's loves, other people's hopes, wishes, supplications. I could read, I suppose. Reading is a way of walking through the world, a walk accessible to those without legs or the liberty to use them. But like that other scrivener, I prefer not to. There is enough reading in the dreams.

Sometimes circumstances make us kill the one we love.
Sometimes circumstances kill the one we love.
Sometimes circumstances make us kill love.
Sometimes circumstances kill love.

I keep trying, but I cannot get the formula right, no matter how long I lie awake at night, no matter how often the phrases repeat themselves in my sleep. It is like the dream reading. I start again and again, tell it in as many different ways as I can, but I cannot escape the point of incomprehension, the point at which everything loses sense, and I have to go back and begin again. Something happened. Something too large perhaps even for a story. I cannot say what it is, but I cannot stop trying.

Dream reading, dream writing, call it what you will, this is what we all do, all our lives long, as we try to impose a pattern on things, to make them fit an acceptable narrative arc. Each time, we believe we are moving out of chaos into meaning, each time we hope sense is going to coalesce; but no matter how neatly structured the narrative, no matter how apt the style, no matter how well chosen the form, meaning always disintegrates, fails to match the truth we are striving after, forcing us back to begin again, on the same page, still dreaming, still reading, still writing, still feeling our way forward, still telling stories. Optimists despite our pessimism, we know things fall apart, but still we start again.

Miss Kate. I miss Kate now. For a while we were sitting on top of the world, but now she is gone, her and all her idealism stifled by the treacherous hands of a loving savior. Perhaps, though, some small part of her person lingers inside me, transferred during the loving or the living or the killing. I wrote earlier of the proper ascription of blame. Those are Kate's words, not mine, white words of guilt and punishment. Is she still present? Is she within me, talking white talk of right and wrong, telling the world where it has gone awry? I do not know. This I do know, though. It is possible to kill one's love, but one cannot kill the love itself. Love stays, a stubborn guest that will not go away. And it hurts. Yet I am obliged to live with my immovable love and the memory of what I did in its name, obliged to pretend that I am still a coherent, functioning human being, because there is Mara. Only she stands between me and the abyss, she and, perhaps, these words. You cannot bring back what you have killed, unless with a story. Stories, like paths, allow us to trace someone absent, they preserve a moment in eternity. Mere preservation is not enough, though. Writing is memory, reading is memory rescued, but it cannot be rescued until the writer has let it go. A written story is a kind of cocoon and, no matter how well crafted, it stays that way until it is read. Then, if you are lucky, if it is read well, if only by a single person who understands the trick of it, it becomes something beautiful and takes wing. With these words, I want my love to be remembered, rescued, to take wing, to live again. It is a kind of redemption, but one that requires complicity. Help me. I have done my bit. I am no more. I want only that my Kate live in an eternal present. The story is not done. It is just beginning. It is for you to make it live.

OK, let's go please.

OTHER TITLES BY CHARLES DAVIS

WALK ON, BRIGHT BOY
144 pp. • 978-1-57962-153-7 • $26 cloth

"A haunting, Gothic novel of a Spaniard, whose horrifying encounters with humanity during the ruthless Inquisition would seem reason to lose faith. But it is also an assertion of spirituality and speaks to contemporary collusions of political expediency and religious faith."

—*ForeWord Magazine*

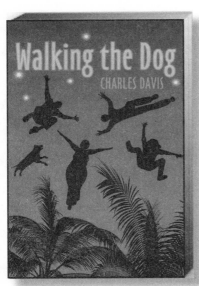

WALKING THE DOG
164 pp. • 978-1-57962-167-4 • $16 paperback

"An episodic, antic romp with outrageous humor, much of it metaphorically sexual; pointed criticism (particularly on water boarding, globalization, spiritualism, elections, and retirement communities) and highly literate prose: the Marx Brothers meet the *Oxford English Dictionary*."

—*The Independent*